"Is it okay that your stockings turn me on?"

Dax had to laugh when Amber squirmed and looked defensive.

"They're more comfortable than regular nylons," she said.

"Thank God for comfort." He stroked his hands down her hips, past her thighs, to the hem of her skirt, then skimmed them back up again, beneath the material now, to...ah, those legs.

She shifted again. "They don't seem to snag like the others—"

"And thriftiness, too." At the feel of lace, then soft bare thighs, he groaned.

"They're very practical, you know," she murmured.

He laughed. "Why don't you just enjoy the reaction you're getting from me...." He slid his hips to hers and lowered his lips to her ear. "Feel what you do to me."

She gripped him tight and nodded.

"More, Amber?"

"Yes, please," she whispered politely, making him crack up again. He'd never in his life laughed while trying to get a woman naked.

Dear Reader,

Have you ever looked into a stranger's eyes and somehow known he was special? Maybe even experienced a bit of love at first sight?

Imagine being trapped in a building, in the dark, utterly unable to get out or even see the hand in front of your face. Imagine being trapped like that with a perfect stranger you've never seen, a man with a voice that could melt the Arctic. A man who has the ability to protect you and keep you from panicking in the face of certain death.

This is what happens to Amber in *Aftershock*, this month's Temptation HEAT. She is not a woman who trusts easily, and certainly not a woman to share her heart, but something inside her changes the day she gets stuck with Daxton McCall, something she can't forget.

I love to hear from readers. You can write me at P.O. Box 3945, Truckee, CA 96160

Happy reading!

Jill Shalvis

P.S. In January, look for my next Temptation book, which will be part of the RED HOT ROYALS miniseries!

AFTERSHOCK
Jill Shalvis

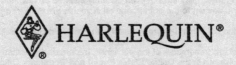

HARLEQUIN®

TORONTO • NEW YORK • LONDON
AMSTERDAM • PARIS • SYDNEY • HAMBURG
STOCKHOLM • ATHENS • TOKYO • MILAN • MADRID
PRAGUE • WARSAW • BUDAPEST • AUCKLAND

ISBN 0-373-25945-X

AFTERSHOCK

Copyright © 2001 by Jill Shalvis.

Visit us at www.eHarlequin.com

Printed in U.S.A.

THE PLACE wasn't what she expected. Though she was alone, Amber Riggs kept her features carefully schooled so that nothing in her cool, serene expression reflected dismay. Control was everything. A deal couldn't be made to the best advantage without it, and she did love a good deal.

She got out of her car without checking her makeup or hair. She didn't need to. It wasn't vanity that told her she looked crisp and businesslike. It was just fact. Her careful facade was purposely created with clothes and makeup so that people took her seriously.

If she were vain, she'd still be basking in the glow from the write-up she'd received in this morning's paper: "A go-get-'em real estate manager." "Best in San Diego county." "No one gets the better of Amber Riggs."

Great for business, but the praise meant little. Amber loved her work, and because she did, she didn't need anyone's approval.

That's what she told herself.

She looked at the deserted warehouse in front of her and frowned. As good at her job as she was, making money from this building would be like bleeding a turnip. It was too far out of town.

Still, stranger things had been known to happen. At least the owner hadn't cared whether she found a buyer or a renter, and that would give her some options.

Her heels clicked noisily on the rough asphalt as she moved closer. The place was two stories and mostly brick, which gave it definite character. That was good. So was the basement that held the offices. She had to sigh as she noted the deterioration of the roof and the decay of the old brick walls. That wasn't good. And no windows, which meant that the client she'd contacted this morning, the one who wanted to convert an older building into an antique mall, wouldn't be happy.

She could fix that, Amber decided, by going inside and finding *something* interesting. Something that would appeal. This was her forte, turning the negative into the positive. Her fat bank account could attest to that. For a girl who'd left home exceptionally early with nothing but the shirt on her back, she'd done okay.

She took the key out of her purse and let herself in. Darkness prevailed, but always prepared, she again reached into her purse for the small flashlight she kept there. As she flipped it on and moved past the reception area into the even darker open warehouse, the silence settled on her shoulders eerily. She swallowed hard, losing a fraction of her iron-clad control.

The dark was not her friend. It was an old fear, from childhood, where she'd spent far too much time alone, afraid. Unwanted.

Dammit, not the self-pity again. She was twenty-seven years old. Maudlin thoughts about her past were unacceptable, and she promptly pushed them aside. Her flashlight shimmered, cutting a path across the huge empty place. The beam hardly made a dent in the absolute blackness, and more of her control slipped. Her palms became damp.

Determinedly, she lifted her chin, letting her logic and famed concentration take over. She was a grown-up. Yes, she was alone, but she wasn't leaving until she'd scoped out the place carefully. She needed something to lure her potential client.

She wanted the deal.

She made it three quarters of the way across the place when she came to a door. Stairs, leading down. Good, the offices there would be a good selling point. Swallowing her discomfort around the intense, inky blackness, she bravely wielded her flashlight and went down the stairs, entering another large and even darker room.

A damp, musty smell greeted her.

An unnatural silence beat down, so did a terrible, heavy foreboding. In the strange stillness, Amber's every nerve ending froze, rendering her incapable of movement.

In the distance, she thought she heard a male voice call out, but that couldn't be, she was alone.

Always alone.

Suddenly a sound like savage thunder ripped through the room, and Amber decided to hell with control. To hell with the deal.

She wanted out.

That's when the earthquake hit.

The unexpected violent pitch and roll of the ground beneath her threw her to the floor, hard. The earth came alive like some monster clawing its way out of hibernation.

Time ceased to exist.

The earth moaned and rocked. As she slid across the cold, concrete floor, her ears rang with the deafening sound. Her skin crawled with horror.

Then she slammed into an unforgiving wall.

Stars exploded into the darkness.

And the last thing Amber heard was her own terrified, piercing scream.

DAX MCCALL loved driving. Loved the freedom of the wind ripping through his hair, the scent of autumn as the trees turned. Loved the eye-squinting azure sky.

Hell, he was feeling generous, he simply loved life.

The tune-up he'd done on his truck the night before had it running smoothly, and he took the time to enjoy the way it handled the unpredictable mountain roads of Point Glen.

He couldn't have asked for a better day. Mother Nature loved Southern California, specifically San

Diego county, and though it was nearly November, the breeze blew warm. Not a cloud marred the brilliant sky. And thanks to the Santa Ana winds, smog was nonexistent, leaving the air unusually clean and pure.

Sunday. His first day off in weeks. Not that he was complaining, he thought, cranking up the rock 'n' roll blaring from the stereo. He loved his job, and knew he was the best damn fire inspector this county had ever seen. But the hours were ruthless, and ambitious as he was, even he needed brain-rest once in awhile.

The last few fires had really taken their toll. He'd just closed an arson case that had spanned two years and caused five deaths. Sometimes at night Dax would close his eyes and see the charred bodies. Worse, he could still see the expression on the family's faces when he'd questioned them. Horror. Pain. Accusation. Sorrow.

Yeah, he needed a day off. Maybe even a vacation. He thought about the wildfires raging out of control in Montana. He could take some time and go help fight them. Not what most would consider a vacation, but in his heart, Dax was first and foremost a firefighter. When he'd turned investigator, he'd never given up his love of fighting fires. Every chance he got, he went back to it.

A shrill ring shattered the peace. *Damn.* Dax turned down the music and answered his cell phone with all the enthusiasm of a child facing bedtime.

"Better be good," he warned, slowing his truck on the narrow two-lane highway as he came into a hairpin turn.

"Some greeting."

Shelley, the oldest of his five nosy, overbearing, sentimental, affectionate sisters, had only one reason for calling.

"The answer is no," Dax said.

Undeterred, she laughed. "Dax, honey, you don't even know what I want."

"Oh, yes, I do." But he had to smile because he loved her. He loved all his sisters, even if they drove him crazy. "It just involves a teensy, weensy favor, right? Just a teensy, weensy *desperate* favor—for a friend?"

"She's not *desperate*."

Yeah, right. "We've discussed this, remember? No more setting me up." He'd told each of his well-meaning, meddling, older sisters that he refused to go out on any more blind dates.

So he was thirty-two and not married, it didn't bother him any. It wasn't as if he hurt for female companionship. But still, his sisters hounded him with friends. And friends of friends. And sisters of friends of friends.

He'd put his foot down long ago, but in their eyes he was still the baby of the family. A six-foot-two-inch, one-hundred-and-eighty pounder with the physique of a man who'd been a firefighter for nearly ten years before he'd become inspector.

Some baby.

"I've got to go, Shel," he said, cradling the phone between his ear and shoulder as he maneuvered the winding road.

"No, you don't. You just don't want me to bug you. Come on, Dax, your last date looked like a twenty-something Dolly Parton and spoke in that stupid whisper no one could understand."

He felt only mildly defensive. Why dispute the truth? So he was partial to blondes. Buxom blondes. Buxom, bubbly blondes, and last he'd checked, there wasn't a law against that. "Hey, I don't bug you about your dates."

"That's because I'm married!"

"You know what? I've got to go." He simulated the sound of static through his teeth. "Bad connection."

"Where are you?" she shouted, which made him grin and feel guilty at the same time.

"On Route 2, by the old mill." Dax frowned as he slowed. Up ahead was the milling plant and warehouse. Isolated from town by at least ten miles and surrounded by woods, the place served little purpose.

It hadn't been used in years. The land was on his list of dangerous properties, a potential disaster just waiting to happen. It was his job to keep properties such as these vacant of homeless people, mischievous teens and desperate lovers.

A small, sleek sports car was parked in front of it, empty. "Dammit."

"Dax McCall!"

"Sorry." He pulled into the lot. "Gotta go, Shel."

"No, don't you dare hang up on me—"

He disconnected and chuckled. She'd stew over that for at least half an hour before calling him back. Long enough, he decided as he got out of the truck, for him to hassle whoever was snooping where they shouldn't.

The door to the building was locked, with no sign of damage or break in, which meant the trespasser had a key.

A real-estate agent.

He knew this with sudden certainty and shook his head in disgust. The bricks were crumbling. Some were missing. The place could collapse with one good gust of wind.

Who could possibly want to buy it?

And why would anyone go wandering around in it? Muttering to himself, he pounded on the door, waiting to face whatever idiot had decided to go into an unsafe building.

No one answered.

Curious now, Dax walked all the way around the building, calling out as he went, but only silence greeted him. Even the woods seemed empty on this unseasonably warm autumn day.

With a resigned sigh, he moved back around to the

front, and examined the weak lock. "Juvenile," he decided with disgust for whoever the owners were.

With a pathetic barrier like this, they were asking for trouble. It took him less than thirty seconds to break in. The large door creaked noisily as he thrust it open and peered inside. "Hello?"

Complete darkness and a heavy mustiness told him there was little to no cross ventilation, which probably meant no alternative exit.

It was every bit as bad as he'd thought—a hazardous nightmare.

He propped open the front door with a rock and entered. If no one answered in the next minute, he'd go back to his truck for a flashlight, but he figured by now, whoever had been inside would be more than happy to get out.

"County Fire Inspector," he called loud and clear. "Come out, this place is dangerous."

A door opened on the far side of the warehouse, and he frowned. "Hey—"

The door slammed. Swearing, he ran toward it, yanked it open.

Stairs.

Far below, he saw the flicker of a light and swore again. "Wait!" He stepped into the stairwell, angry at himself now for not stopping to get his own flashlight, because he couldn't see a thing. "Stop!"

Those were the last words he uttered before the quake hit, knocking him to his butt on the top steel stair.

Born and raised in Southern California, Dax had experienced many quakes before. He considered himself seasoned. Still, it was unsettling to be leveled flat without warning, his ears echoing with the roar of the earth as it rocked and rolled beneath him.

The shaking went on and on and on, and he lost his bearings completely. He could see nothing, which disoriented him, and he hated that. Beneath him, the stairs rattled and shook violently. He held onto the rail for all he was worth, not even attempting to stand.

"Don't give," he begged as he clenched onto the steel for dear life. "Just don't give, baby."

At least a six-point-zero, he decided with some detachment, as he waited for the world to right itself again.

But it didn't. He upgraded mentally to a six-point-five.

He heard a roar, then the crash of tumbling bricks, which was a bad thing.

Very bad.

As he ducked his head to his knees, protecting the back of his neck with his hands, heavy debris tumbled down around him.

A new fear gripped him then—the building couldn't withstand the movement. The whole thing was going to go and, in the process, so was he.

Dax prayed fervently for the place, mostly the staircase that he sat clinging to, hoping, hoping, hoping, but with a sick feeling in the pit of his stomach.

He knew the ancient building couldn't hold up to this kind of jarring.

It was going to collapse and there were two floors above him.

Dead meat sitting, that's what he was.

A metallic taste filled his mouth and he realized he'd bitten his tongue, hard. Half expecting his life to flash before his eyes, Dax was surprised that all he could think of was his family. They wouldn't know where to find his body, and that would destroy his mother.

His sisters would never be able to set him up again.

Then the bottom dropped out from beneath his world, and he fell.

And fell.

As he did, he heard a scream.

2

DAX LANDED HARD, on his already bruised butt.

The hit jarred him senseless for a moment, and the all-consuming dark further confused him. He remembered the destruction of the stairwell he'd been on and knew that meant big trouble when it came to getting out.

He also remembered the scream.

"Hello! Fire inspector," he called out roughly. In the blackness, he quickly rose to his knees, then coughed and gagged on a deep breath of dust and dirt.

Not being able to see, he felt disoriented, but his professional training and innate need to help others quickly cleared his head. "*Hello?*"

"Over here!"

Female. *Hell*, he thought, scrambling as fast as he could over what felt like mountains of brick and steel. The collapsed stairwell, he realized. "I'm coming!" His lungs burned. "Where are you?"

"Here." He heard her choke and sputter on the same dirt he'd inhaled. "Here!" she cried louder, just as he reached out and touched her leg.

"Oh!" Clearly startled, she pulled back.

But Dax was determined, and afraid for her. Had any of the falling debris struck her? Gently but firmly, he closed in, and feeling his way, streaked his hands over her.

She made an unintelligible sound.

"Where are you hurt?" he asked. Without waiting for an answer, he carefully and methodically checked her arms, silently cursing his lack of a flashlight. He ran his hands over her legs, during which he had the thought that even a saint—something he most definitely wasn't—would have recognized what a fine set of legs they were. Long, lean, toned and bare except for a silky pair of stockings.

"Hey, stop that!" Hands slapped at him, and when he got to her hips, she went wild, scooting back and kicking out.

He caught a toe on his chin.

A toe that was covered in a high heel pump, if he wasn't mistaken. And for the second time in so many minutes, he saw stars. "Stop, I won't hurt you," he told her in the same calming, soothing voice he'd used to placate hundreds of victims. No broken bones, thank God.

"Back off then."

"In a minute." He gripped her narrow waist in his big hands. "Are your ribs okay?"

"Yes! Now get your paws off me while I find my damn flashlight." She shifted away from him, and then promptly let out a low, pained gasp at her movement.

Immediately he was there, reaching for her. "Let me," he demanded quietly, running his hands up her waist, over each individual rib with precision and care. Nothing broken there, except his own breathing because there was something inexplicably erotic about touching a woman he'd never seen. Though he couldn't see her, he sure could feel her, and she was something; all feminine curves, soft skin and sweet, enticing scent.

He felt her cross her arms over her chest, and as a result, the back of his knuckles brushed against the plumped flesh of her breasts.

At the contact, she made a strangled sound, then shoved him. "Not there!"

Her shoulders seemed fine, if a little petite, so did both arms, but he could feel the telltale stickiness on one of her elbows, which he'd missed before. Maybe it had just started bleeding.

Everything else vanished as his training took over. "You've cut yourself." Concern filled him because they were dirty, with no immediate way out, and he had no first-aid kit. Infection was imminent.

"I'm fine."

Her fierce independence made her seem all the more vulnerable, and as all victims seemed to do, she tugged at something deep inside him. So did her cool voice, because in direct contrast to that, he could feel her violent trembling. He ripped a strip of material off his T-shirt and tied it around her arm to protect the cut from more dirt.

She was still shaking.

"You okay?" Damn, he wished he could see her. If she went into shock, there was little he could do for her, and the helplessness of it all tore at him.

"I just want out of here," she said, slightly less icily then before.

"Are you cold? Let me—" He reached for her, but she shifted away.

"I told you, I'm fine."

It amazed him how calm she sounded. Dax's sisters were all equally loved, but also equally spoiled rotten. They were never quiet, *never* calm. And certainly never in control. If a fingernail broke, if it rained on a new hairstyle, if Brad Pitt got married, the world came to an end.

It wasn't a stretch for Dax to admit that the women he dated—and since women were a weak spot for him, he dated a lot—were much the same.

But this woman in front of him, the one he couldn't see, could only feel, was an enigma to him.

Again, she pushed away.

He heard her struggle to her feet. "Hey, careful," he urged.

"I'm not going to faint."

The disdain in her voice told him what she thought of *that* particular weakness.

"I'm not," she added to his silence. "I had a flashlight. I want it now."

At that queen-to-peasant voice, he had to laugh. "Well, then. By all means, let me help you find it."

Stretching out, he felt his way along the floor, painstakingly searching for the light with his fingers. "You're a hell of a cool cucumber, you know."

"It was just an earthquake."

"Yeah well, that was one hell of an earthquake."

"Do you always swear?"

"Yes, but I'll try to control myself." His back to her, he closed his fingers over the flashlight. Though the bulb flickered and was nearly dead, it came on.

Looking at the situation before him, he let out a slow breath and swore again.

Coming up behind him, she made a sound of impatience. "I thought you were going to control yourself— *Oh*." She paused. "This isn't good."

"No." Grim reality settled on his shoulders like a solid weight as he surveyed the situation in the faint light before him. "Not good at all."

The stairway was completely destroyed, lying in useless piles around them. There was no other entry into the basement where they stood, except the hole far above them. On the ground, directly beneath that opening, was a huge mountain of fallen brick and steel.

The pile previously known as the staircase.

There was no way out. They were literally buried alive.

"The entire building...it's gone, isn't it?" she asked softly, still behind him.

Dax thought about lying. It would protect her and his first instinct was always to protect and shelter, at any cost. But he already knew she wasn't a woman to be coddled. "Looks that way."

"We're going to die."

So calm, so matter-of-fact, even when he knew she had to be terrified. "We still have oxygen," he said positively. "And the flashlight."

That was when the damn light died.

In stunned silence, she drew an audible deep breath.

Reaching behind him, he groped for her hand. Surprisingly, she took it and held on.

"If the quake hadn't slid us across the floor, away from the opening," she said, her voice very sober, very small, "We'd be toast right now."

Burnt toast, Dax thought, gently squeezing her fingers.

"Well, we're not dead yet."

Maybe not, but they would be soon enough. Tons of brick lay on top of the thin ceiling of the basement above their heads. They'd been saved only by the dubious strength of that protection. Dax had no idea how long the floor would hold. He didn't imagine it could withstand the inevitable aftershock.

"Does someone know where you are?" he asked, carefully keeping his growing shock and dismay to himself.

"No." Through their joined hands, he felt her shiver again.

He'd been in some hairy situations before, it was the nature of his job. He was good at saving his own behind, even better at saving others, but he thought maybe his luck had just run out.

Regret and rage threatened to consume him, but he wasn't ready to give up yet. He drew in a ragged breath and nearly gagged on the lingering dust. "Come on, this is the hallway, there must be more rooms. They'll be far cleaner than this, it'll be easier to breathe." And maybe there would be some sort of steel-lined safe they could crowd into for protection when the ceiling over their head collapsed, assuming they had enough oxygen to wait for rescue.

"There's two offices, a bathroom and a small kitchenette," she intoned. "Furnished." She shrugged, her shoulder bumping against his. "I have the listing in my pocket."

Dax wished the flashlight hadn't gone out, wished that he'd gotten a look at the woman next to him before it had, wished that he'd eaten more for breakfast that morning than a bowl of Double Chocolate Sugary O's.

"We'll be fine." She sounded secure, confident, despite her constant shivers. "We'll just wait to be rescued. Right?"

Dax decided to let her have that little fantasy since he wasn't ready to face the alternative, though he held no illusions—when the weight of the crumbled two stories above them came through the ceiling, they were as good as dead.

Feeling their way through the inky darkness, climbing and struggling, they left the hallway. It wasn't fast or easy, and Dax kept waiting for the woman to falter or complain, or fall apart.

But to his amazement, she never did.

They decided they were in one of the offices, which after a bit of fumbling around, they discovered had a couch, a desk, two chairs and some other unidentifiable equipment. The second office was smaller, and from what they could tell, void of furniture. The kitchenette seemed dangerous, the floor was littered with fallen appliances and a tipped-over refrigerator.

There was no safe place to hide except back in the first office. Like a trooper, the woman stoically kept up with him as they made their way. He couldn't help but wonder at her incredible control, and what had made her that way.

A DISTANT rumbling was their only warning, but it was enough for Amber, who reacted without thinking by throwing herself at the stranger who'd become her entire world. Later she'd be mortified by her lack of control, but at the moment control was the *last* thing on her mind.

As the earth once again pitched and rolled beneath their feet, the man snatched her closer and sank with her to the floor.

"Hurry," he demanded, pushing her under what felt like a huge, wooden desk. He crawled in after her.

She had time to think the earth's movement was

slight compared to the other quake before he hauled her beneath him, sprawling his big and—*oh my*—very tough body over hers, protecting her head by crushing it to his chest.

Time once again ceased to exist as she closed her eyes and lived through the aftershock. Huddled in the pitch dark, Amber knew what the man holding her so tightly feared—as she feared—death. It could easily happen, right this second, and she waited breathlessly for the ceiling above them to give and crush them.

Unwilling to die, she held on, reacting instinctively by burrowing closer to the stranger's warmth, his strength. He had both in spades and shared it freely.

After what seemed like years—she'd lost all sense of time—the rocking stopped.

She became aware of how close they were. How big a man he was, how every inch of her was plastered to every inch of him. *A stranger.*

She'd thrown herself at a stranger.

Mortified, she pushed at him. Immediately, he rolled off her and they lay there beneath the desk, separated by inches. Holding their breath.

Nothing crushed them. In fact, the silence was so complete it was nothing short of eerie.

"It held," she whispered.

"Yeah." In the dark he shifted, and she got the feeling he was staring at her. "You're incredible, you know that?"

No one had ever called her such a thing before. "Why?"

"You're so calm. No panic."

"You didn't panic," she pointed out.

"Yeah, but..."

"But I'm a woman?"

"I'm sorry." There was a reluctant smile in his voice. "But yes, because you're a woman I guess I expected you to wig out over that one."

With hard won habit and sheer will, she never wigged out. Not Amber Riggs. She had too much control for that. The master himself had taught her the art. Her father had demanded perfection from her, and total submission.

He'd gotten it.

The fact that her cold, hard, exacting military parent could still intrude on her life, especially at a time like this, where every last moment counted, really infuriated her. She shoved the unhappy memories aside.

"I like control," she said, and if her voice was tinged with steely determination, she couldn't help it. She was proud of her cool, sophisticated front. It certainly hadn't come easily. How many times had she been told she mustn't be like the mother she'd never known? The mother who'd been wild and uncontrollable before she'd taken off after Amber's birth?

A slut, her father liked to remind his daughter.

No, Amber must never be like her.

Little chance of that when she'd grown up with no maternal influence to soften her strict, unbending father. Once upon a time, she'd done everything in her power to earn his approval, but it had never come. She'd learned to live without it.

She didn't need his, or *anyone's*, approval.

As a result, her life was quiet, and okay, maybe a bit sterile, but she'd convinced herself that was how she wanted it. She didn't need anyone or anything, and she especially didn't need what she secretly felt unworthy of—*love*.

Instead, she buried herself in the one thing that would never hurt or disappoint her—her work—and she liked it that way.

So what was that stab of regret she felt now, while she lay waiting to die? What was this terrible sadness coursing through her, this certainty that by ignoring all emotion and passion in order to succeed at her work, she'd somehow let life pass her by?

She was single; no husband, no children. Not even a boyfriend or a casual date. A barren woman with a barren life.

What would it be like to have a man waiting for her right now, worrying over her? Loving her with all his heart and soul?

She'd never know now.

Another rumbling came.

Before she could react, the stranger was there, again yanking her close into the heat and safety of his arms. He had big, warm hands and they settled at her back, soothing and protective.

This quake felt much slighter, a huge relief. But it allowed other things to crowd Amber's brain besides fear.

Things like the man she was glued to.

She could feel the fierce pounding of his heart, feel his large hands gently cup her head, feel the tough sinew of his hard body as it surrounded hers. The weirdest sensation flooded her.

Arousal, she realized in shock.

Good Lord, one little emergency and she started acting like her mother!

She couldn't believe it, and promptly blamed the circumstances for her shocking lack of control. But the connection between her and this man felt like ice and fire at once, and it baffled her. *Danger*, she told herself. It was just the danger, the sense of impending death making her feel like this, all liquidy and...well, hot.

"It's okay," he whispered in that incredible voice, the one that made her feel like melted butter.

She couldn't have it, *wouldn't* have it, and yet she couldn't seem to let go of him. A whimper sounded, and she was horrified to realize it was her own.

Needing to be free, she fought him.

"Shh, you're all right," he told her when she struggled against both him and the unaccustomed feelings swimming through her. With frightening ease, he lay her back on the ground, easily subduing her.

Above them came the booming sound of more falling brick, and it was louder, more terrifying than Amber could imagine. The falling debris hit the top of the desk that was protecting them, nearly startling her right out of her own skin.

They were going to die now.

She had to get out. But she couldn't budge, he held her too close, protecting her body with his.

"Don't fight me," he coaxed in her ear. "We've got to stay right here."

"No," she gasped, wrestling, listening to the noise of the building crumbling to dust around them, feeling the heat of him as he held her safe no matter how she fought him.

Didn't he understand? She'd lost it, her prized control was gone, and the greater danger lay right here, in his warm, strong arms. "I need out!" she cried.

"You can't." Regret made his voice harsh, but so did determination as he leaned over her, cuffing her hands over her head, restraining her with his superior strength.

"Listen," he demanded as she silently fought him with everything she had. "Listen to me!" He gave her a little shake. "The building has collapsed on top of us. If you leave the safety of the desk now, when the ceiling of this basement gives..."

Not *if* the ceiling collapses, but *when.* He didn't have to finish his sentence, but God, oh God, she couldn't bear it, this enforced contact between them.

She was plastered to him from head to toe and the opaque blackness only added to the sense of intimacy.

"It's stopped," he murmured, relieved, and she felt his cheek brush against hers. "It's over."

She waited with what she considered admirable patience, but he didn't let her go. "Get off me."

"Promise me you won't do something stupid."

Stupid. Oh, that was good. They were going to die when she'd never really even lived. She had nothing to show for her life, nothing except for what would soon be a useless bank account. Now *that* was stupid. "Let me up."

"Not until you promise you won't disturb the balance of things."

Still helplessly stretched out beneath him, she shifted and discovered he had one powerful leg between hers. Every time she moved, the core of her came in contact with the juncture of his thighs.

She'd been too busy trying to get free to pay much attention, but suddenly she realized she wasn't the only one who was affected by their closeness.

He was aroused.

He was actually hard, for *her*. It seemed so absolutely amazing. Surreal.

Later she would blame age-old instincts, but whatever it was, it made her hips arch slightly.

In response, he made a dark sound that shot an arrow of heat straight through her. *This was life*, came the insane thought.

Go for it. Take it.

She moved against him again, tentatively.

He muttered something; a curse, a prayer, she had no idea which, and at the sound, blind desire overcame her. Before she could stifle the urge, she pressed even closer.

"Your name," he demanded, letting go of her hands to slide his down her arms. "I need to know your name."

"Amber."

"Daxton McCall. Dax." His hands came up now to cup her face, and a callused thumb brushed over her lips, so lightly she wasn't sure if she imagined it, but it gave her a jolt of awareness that was almost painful.

Suddenly her world was rocking and she was no longer certain if it was another earthquake or just reaction to the insane sexiness of his voice, his body.

"You're shaking," he whispered.

She couldn't stop.

"Let me warm you." Gently, tenderly, he scooped her closer, running those big, sure hands over her spine to her hips, bringing her tight against his delicious heat...his incredible erection.

It was wrong to sigh over it; so very, very wrong, snuggling up to a man she'd never even seen. A stranger for God's sake.

But for the life of her, she couldn't pull away.

She needed this, desperately. Needed this reaffirmation that they were indeed alive, at least for now.

She was going to live life to the fullest, she promised herself. Every second she had left.

But as a huge thundering crash echoed around them, she couldn't help but scream.

The walls shook, the ceiling shuddered, and they clung together, holding their breath, waiting, waiting, each second an eternity.

No more chances. This was it.

They were going to die.

3

TERRIFIED, Amber cried out for her stranger, her Dax McCall. She had no idea what she wanted to say, but in that moment, with their world coming apart, it didn't matter.

He understood. "I'm here, right here," he told her, his body close so she couldn't forget.

"It's so loud," she cried, horrified at how weak she sounded.

"You're not alone."

"I'm scared."

"Me, too."

"I need..."

"I know. I do, too. Come here, come closer." And he enclosed her in a tight embrace that was so erotically charged, she could almost forget she lay huddled beneath a desk on cheap flannel carpeting in the basement of a building that had collapsed above them.

Her face was buried in his neck, and because it was so warm, so indelibly male, she left it there, inhaling deeply the very masculine scent of him. "We're going to die," she said against his skin.

She felt him shake his head.

His denial was sweet, but she didn't want to be protected, not from this. "Tell me the truth."

"I don't want to believe it."

"Neither do I." It was unlike her to talk to a stranger, much less cling to one. Even more unlike her to admit to her real feelings on anything. But the words poured from her lips before she could stop them. "I don't want it to end like this. It can't. I've never really lived, not once, it can't be too late!"

He didn't say anything about the loss of her calm, cool sophistication, for which she thought she might be forever grateful. In fact, he didn't say anything at all, he just continued to touch her, maintaining the connection between them.

"Dax, I think—"

"Don't think."

"But there's so much—"

"*Don't.*"

"I can't stop. I can't turn it off."

"You're shaking again." In his voice was a wealth of concern and compassion, two emotions sorely missing in her life. He worried. He didn't even know her, and he worried. Just thinking about it had her eyes misting.

How was it that a stranger could care so much for her in such a short time, when no one else ever had?

That was her own fault, and she knew it. Another regret. She didn't let people in, didn't let people care. Things had to change.

Starting right now. "I want to live."

"You're thinking again."

"I can't stop."

"Let me help."

"Yes." *Anything.*

"Try this..." He angled her head up and met her lips with his.

Far above them, the ceiling groaned and strained under the weight of debris. The ominous, ever-present creaking got louder.

In opposition to Amber's surging, very real fear, Dax's kiss was soft, gentle, sweet.

"Stay with me," he whispered against her lips.

His warm, giving mouth was heaven, such absolute heaven, that she gradually did just as he asked, she stayed with him, lost herself in him, drowning in the very new sensation of desire and passion.

A sound escaped her, a mere whisper of the pleasure starting to thread through her body. He soothed and assured, both with that magical voice and even more magical hands, kissing her again and again, until shyly, eagerly, she opened to him, only to jerk at the resounding thunder of more falling debris.

"Shh, I'm here," he murmured, then dipped his head again.

The shock of his tongue curling around hers was a welcome one, and Amber pressed closer, grateful, desperate for more of the delicious distraction. One of his hands continued to cup her face, stroking her skin, the other drifted down her body, curving over her bottom, squeezing. He rocked her slowly, purposely, against his hips.

But when the ceiling made yet another terrible straining sound, she cringed.

"No, don't listen to that." Now his clever mouth was at her ear, his words sparking little shivers down her spine. "Stay with me, remember?"

As their world crumbled around them, Dax was right there, commanding her attention, drawing her out of her fear. "Listen to the blood pound through your body," he murmured, pressing his lips to her temple. "Listen to the sound of our breathing...do you hear it? Do you?" he urged, willing her to let go of the terror to concentrate on what he was making her feel.

It worked, and when she felt his hot, wet mouth on her skin, she gasped and arched up into him.

"Listen to your body craving mine...."

Oh yes, yes she heard it now, the blood whipping through her system as he tasted her. She heard the sound of his low, rough groan when she writhed against him. Knowing she was causing his harsh, ragged breathing gave her an incredible sense of power. "More," she begged. "Help me forget that we're going to—"

Die, she'd been about to say, but he simply swallowed the word and kissed it away. He kissed her mouth, her face, her throat, all the while using his hands to stoke the fire. Her blouse fell open beneath his hands, and he treated her breasts to the same glo-

rious magic, sucking and nibbling and stroking her
nipples until she begged for more.

The rest happened so fast that afterward she could
never fully recall it except as a hazy, sensuous,
haunting dream. She tore open his jeans; he shoved
them off his hips. He slid his hands up her skirt,
groaning when he came to her thigh-high stockings,
her one secret luxury. She might have spared a moment for embarrassment, but then he whipped off
her panties and slipped his fingers between her
thighs, dipping into her wet heat. Touching, stroking, claiming her until she couldn't think of anything
but getting more.

Penetration wasn't easy, it had been a pathetically
long time for her, but Dax slowed, teasing her aching, swollen flesh with his knowing fingers until she
was ready to take him. He was huge, hot and throbbing inside her. Unbearably aroused, Amber tossed
her head back, lifted her hips and sobbed as unfa-
miliar sensations rocketed through her. She was on
the very edge, teetering, madly trying to regain her
balance, but he didn't allow it.

"Let it happen," he whispered, his fingers teasing
and urging and tormenting. "Come for me, Amber.
Come for me now."

The pleasure was so intense she couldn't have
held back if she'd wanted to. She was wild, completely out of herself, as the orgasm took her.

And took her.

It was endless. Above her, she felt him convulse,

heard his hoarse cry, then they fell together, trembling, their hearts pounding violently.

Amber had no idea how much time passed before Dax lifted his head and stroked the damp hair from her face. "You okay?"

She thought about it and smiled. "Yes." Crazy as it seemed, she was definitely okay.

Wrung out by their hollowing, grinding, shattering emotions, they dozed then, still locked in each other's arms.

"ARE YOU TAKEN?" The minute the words fell out of her mouth, Amber winced. *Stupid.* And if she hadn't so neatly cut herself off from socializing all these years, she could have done better. "I mean—"

Besides her, Dax laughed softly. "I know what you mean. And no, I'm not married, I never would have made love to you otherwise."

They'd made love. Good Lord.

And they'd had two more aftershocks. They sat side by side, still beneath the desk. Mortified as Amber was over what they'd done, Dax had refused to let her leave the safety of their meager protection.

"Not that I have anything against the institution of marriage in general," he offered. "But I come from a huge family. Five meddling sisters and two equally meddling parents. Ten nieces and nephews. Tons of diapers and messes and wild family dinners." She felt his mock shudder.

It had always been just her father and herself, so

Amber could only imagine the sort of life he described. But family or not, she could understand his need to be alone, uncommitted. She herself was alone most of the time, and greatly preferred it to the alternative. Letting someone in meant letting someone have control over her, which was not an option.

She'd had enough of that to last her a lifetime; first with her father, who'd been almost maniacal in his desire to curb her every impulse, and then she'd repeated the cycle with her ex-fiancé.

She didn't intend to make that mistake again, ever.

"I plan to settle down in another twenty years or so." Dax's voice had a smile in it. "Maybe when I'm forty. Just in time to have a double rocking chair on my porch." Then his amusement faded away. "That's my hope anyway."

If I live.

His unspoken words hung between them. "They'll worry about me," he said after a moment, very softly. "I hate knowing that."

She could hear the deep, abiding love he had for the people he cared about, and wondered what it would be like to know she was unconditionally loved that way.

"How about you?" he asked. "Who do you share your life with? Who's missing you right now, worrying about you?"

She opened her mouth, but had nothing to say.

"What? Too personal?" He let out a little laugh and nudged her. "What could be more personal than what we've already done together? Come on, now. Share.''

''No one.''

''No one what?''

''There's...no one.''

He was quiet for a moment. Probably horrified. ''I have a hard time believing a woman like you has no one in her life,'' he said finally, very gently.

It shocked her, the way he said ''a woman like you.'' His voice held admiration, attraction, tenderness.

Under different circumstances, she might have laughed. The truth was she'd been a wallflower nearly all her life. Only when she'd struck out on her own, ruthlessly devouring magazines and books on fashion and style, had her appearance changed so that no one could actually *see* that wallflower within her. To the world, she appeared cool, elegant, sophisticated.

Apparently she'd fooled him, too.

''Amber?''

''I think you know I don't have a lover,'' she said quietly. ''Not recently anyway.'' She ducked her hot cheeks to rest them against her bent knees. ''No attachments.''

She could feel him studying her. Could feel his curiosity and confusion.

''There's no shame in that.'' He slid a hand up and down her back.

No, maybe not, she thought wearily. But there was

in her memory. "I was engaged once," she admitted. "Several years ago. It didn't work out." She didn't add she'd discovered her fiancé had been hand-picked by her father, drawn to her by the promise of promotion. That Roy had used her to further his military career, instead of really loving her as she'd allowed herself to imagine, had been devastating.

So had her father's involvement.

Of course he'd been bitterly disappointed when she'd backed out of the arrangement. She'd failed him, and he'd made that perfectly clear.

Well, dammit, he'd failed her, too.

After that, Amber had hardened herself. Being alone was best. No involvement, no pain. She believed it with all her shut-off heart.

"I'm sorry." Dax reached for her hand, but at the pity she heard in his voice, she flinched away.

"No, don't," he whispered, scooting closer, feeling for her face to make sure she was looking at him. "I'm sorry you've been hurt, but I'm not sorry you're alone now."

She had no idea what to say to that.

"Don't regret what happened here, between us. I don't."

It was difficult to maintain any sort of distance when the man was continually touching her with both that voice and his hands. He was so compassionate, so giving, and he was doing his absolute best to keep her comfortable, all the while filling her with a traitorous sexual awareness.

For the first time in her life, she wondered if she'd judged her mother too harshly. It wasn't a thought that sat well with her.

"Amber?"

That was another thing about him, he refused to let her hide, even from herself. "I won't regret it," she promised, knowing they were going to die anyway. "It would be a waste to regret something so wonderful."

"Yes, it would."

"I don't want to die." She hadn't meant to say it, but there it was.

The words hung between them.

"The ceiling is holding," he said after a moment. "The desk has protected us."

Yes, but they would be crushed soon enough. The ceiling above them was still making groaning noises and no amount of reassurances or placating lies could cover that up. They knew from Dax's careful exploring that one corner of the office had collapsed under tons of dirt and brick. They now had half the space they'd had originally.

Suddenly Dax froze.

"What—"

Dax put his fingers to her mouth. "Shh." He sat rigidly still, poised, listening. "Hear that?"

She tried. "No."

He surged to his feet, banging his head on the desk. He swore ripely, apologized hastily, then crawled out and shouted.

"What are you doing?" Amber demanded, fear clogging her throat. He'd get hurt, something would fall on him.

She'd be alone.

Always alone.

She didn't want to die that way.

"Someone's up there," he told her with a shocked laugh. "They're looking for us. *Listen!*"

Then she heard it, the unmistakable shouts of people.

Joy surged.

She was going to live after all. She was going to get a second chance.

And thanks to Dax McCall, this time around she'd make the most of it.

IT TOOK HOURS to rescue them from the building, but eventually Amber was standing in the asphalt parking lot, blinking like a mole at the fading daylight.

Hard to believe, but they were okay. They were alive. And while they'd been trapped, life had gone on, business as usual.

Well, not quite. Southern California had suffered a six-point-five earthquake.

Amber turned to look at the small crowd of police officers and firefighters surrounding her perfect stranger, and she suffered her own six-point-five tremor.

Dax McCall was tall, lean and built like a runner. No, like a boxer, she amended, all sinewy and tough.

Big. It was hard to discern the color of his hair, or even the tone of his skin, covered in dust as he was, but to her, he was stunningly, heart wrenchingly gorgeous.

He was her hero, in a world where she'd never had one before.

But that was silly, the stuff movies were made of, and she was mature enough to realize it. He was human, and she had no need for a hero in her life. Nor for a huge, warm, strong, incredibly sexy man. Still, she stood there, pining after him, allowing herself for one moment to daydream.

I plan to settle down, he'd said. *In another twenty years or so.*

She'd do well to remember that.

Yes, this had been an amazing episode in her life— literally soul-shaking. The way he'd held her, touched her, kissed her, as if she'd been the only woman on earth, was something she'd always remember.

But it was over now, and he wouldn't want to cling to the moment. In fact, he was probably already worrying about how to let her down gently.

That wouldn't be necessary.

Oh, he was kind, gentle, tender. Some woman had certainly taught him right. Probably *many* women. But Amber had no desire to be the flavor of the week, and he had no desire for more. He'd made it abundantly clear that he wasn't into commitments. So really, there was only one thing to do, after she thanked him—cut her losses and leave.

Getting him alone proved difficult. Their rescuers had circled him and were deep in conversation, so she waited. Around her was the eerie silence of a regular day. Trees barely moving, sky clear and bright. Little traffic.

But it wasn't a regular day. Suddenly feeling claustrophobic, more than she had while trapped in the basement, Amber knew she couldn't stay another moment. Vowing to thank him in person later, after a hot shower, a good meal and a very private, very rare, pity party, she got into her car.

Taking control of her emotions and actions felt good. Still, her heart gave a painful lurch as she buckled in. Before Dax had finished giving his report to the police, she was gone, assuring herself she was doing the right thing by leaving.

A part of her, though, a very small part, knew the truth. On the outside, to the world, she was tough as nails and cool as a cucumber. Inside, where she allowed no one, she was one big, soft chicken.

And when she put her foot to the accelerator, it was the chicken who ran.

4

One year later:

DAX LED his very pregnant sister off the elevator of the medical center and headed toward the obstetrician's office.

Suzette kept tripping over her own two feet, making him sweat with nerves. She was going to do a swan dive on his poor, unborn nephew or niece, he just knew it. "Please," he begged, holding her arm tight, tempted to sweep her in his arms and carry her himself. "Be careful!"

"You'd trip, too, if you couldn't see your feet." But loving being pregnant, she grinned at him. "Don't worry, I won't go into labor on you."

"I want that in writing," he muttered, glancing at her huge, swollen belly. He'd delivered a baby before, during his firefighting days, when the paramedics hadn't arrived in time. It had been miraculous, awe-inspiring...and terrifying.

"Oh relax." Without mercy, Suzette laughed at him. "I feel great."

"Relaxing around you is impossible."

"Really, I'm fine. Except for a contraction every two minutes."

Now *he* tripped, and she laughed again. "I love you, Dax."

She kept smiling at him, with huge, misty eyes, and he immediately slowed, slapping his pockets for a tissue, knowing from past experiences she was going to get all sappy on him and cry. "Dammit, Suzette."

"I'm fine. Really." But she sniffed and blinked her huge, wet eyes. "You're just so sweet. So much a part of my life. And sometimes I can't help but think about how we almost lost you to that earthquake."

Dax started to shrug it off, but she stopped, planted herself and her big belly in front of him, and said, "Don't act like it doesn't matter, don't you dare. If you hadn't been talking to Shelley just before you stopped to check out that building, no one would have known where you were. We never would have found you in time."

Because she was getting herself worked up, and making him very nervous while doing it, Dax tried to soothe her. "It worked out okay—"

"You know darn well it almost didn't! The ceiling of that basement completely collapsed on itself only an hour after they got you and that woman out."

That woman.

It had taken him all year, but Dax had managed to steel himself against the white-hot stab of regret he always felt at the thought of Amber. The pain had finally, *finally*, started to dissipate.

"What if we hadn't gotten to you in time?" Suzette demanded. "You could have *died*, Dax. And you're my favorite brother."

"I'm your *only* brother."

Suzette just shook her head and sniffed again. But he was tired of obsessing about the earthquake, and what had happened between him and Amber. It had invaded his thoughts, his life, his dreams for too long now. It was over. *Over*.

"Those hormones are really something," he said, but he handed her a tissue. "Aren't you tired of crying yet?"

"Nope, it feels good." A big fat tear rolled down her cheek. "Thanks for driving me here."

"Just as long as Alan makes sure to get off for the birth. I am most definitely not available for the coaching job."

He was teasing her and they both knew it. He'd do anything she needed, and for just an instant, for one insane little spurt in time, Dax thought maybe he wouldn't mind being a coach at all.

"Someday this will be you," she said softly, bringing his hand to her belly so that he could feel the wonder of the baby's movement.

"Not in the near future," he said, but he spread his fingers wide, feeling the miracle beneath; moving, growing, *living*.

"It will be," Suzette promised. "Someday, some

woman is going to snag you, make you forget why you like being single. Trust me on this."

Without warning, the memory of lying huddled beneath a desk, waiting to die, holding the frightened but courageous Amber hit him, hard. That day he'd prepared himself for a hysterical, whiny female, but she had surprised him with her inner strength, her quiet resolve to survive.

He'd been drawn to her on a level he couldn't have imagined. Compared to his wonderful but flighty sisters, and the wild bombshells he had an admittedly bad habit of dating, Amber had seemed like a startling breath of fresh air.

He'd wanted, badly, to see her face, and for the first time in his life, it hadn't been to determine if she was as sexy as her voice. He'd wanted to look into her eyes and see for himself if the connection between them was as real as it felt.

In those terror-filled moments, when they'd been so certain the end had come, they'd come together in the dark; desperate and afraid, hungry and needy, joining together to make unforgettable, perfect love, without ever having set eyes on each other.

It had been poignant, amazing...*necessary*. As necessary as breathing.

The image of Amber exploding in his arms wasn't new; it was never far from his mind. What they'd shared had been incredible, as soul-shattering as the earthquake had been, and he couldn't forget it, no matter how hard he tried.

And yet Amber obviously had.

Despite his best efforts to find her, she'd vanished. He'd gotten an all-too-quick glimpse of her that day, and though she'd been nothing like the women he usually found himself attracted to, he'd thought her short, sleek, dark hair and even darker eyes the most beautiful he'd ever seen.

At first he searched so diligently for her because there was every chance he had gotten her pregnant. That he hadn't used a condom was disturbing, he *always* used protection. But then again, neither of them had expected to live through the experience.

By the time Dax tracked her down—not an easy feat when he hadn't even known her last name— she'd been gone. He'd located her office, only to be told she'd taken a leave of absence. She'd subleased her condo.

No forwarding address.

Inexplicably devastated, Dax had gone to help fight the wildfires in Montana. He'd been there a month, during which time his disgruntled secretary messed up his office good, and then took another job.

When he'd gotten back, there were no messages, but by then he hadn't expected any from Amber.

She was long gone.

Clearly, she'd wanted no reminder of that one day they'd shared, which was fine. He had his own life, which consisted of work, women and fun. He hadn't looked back.

Much.

"Let's sign you in," he said to Suzette now, shaking the memories off. "This place is packed."

AMBER WAS LATE. Her alarm hadn't gone off, she'd annoyed a client by running behind, and now she was stuck in traffic.

Definitely, a terminally bad day.

Normally she'd have felt weighed down by all the stress. She'd have fought it with breathing techniques and her famed cool control.

But fighting wasn't necessary, because none of it was important. Her life had forever changed on that fateful day she'd gotten caught in the earthquake, and now all that mattered was Taylor.

She pulled into the medical center knowing if she didn't rush, she'd be late for their three-month pediatric appointment, and she hated that. She was never late, yet here she was racing through the parking lot with baby Taylor in her arms and a huge diaper bag hanging off her shoulder, hitting her with each stride.

If she'd gotten up on time, she chided herself, she wouldn't be rushing now. But she was always so tired lately. It was all the change, she decided. Becoming a mother. Coming back to town after a year-long...what?

What did one call it when a person ran away from her job, her home, her life?

A *vacation*, she reminded herself firmly. She'd never in her life taken one, certainly she'd been enti-

tled. Just because she'd taken it immediately follow-
ing the earthquake didn't mean it had anything to do
with the choices she'd made.

Neither did one rugged, sexy, unforgettable Dax
McCall.

Nope.

God, what a liar she was. The cooing sound
stopped her cold. Staring down into her daughter's
face, her heart simply tipped on its side.

Baby-blue eyes stared back at her. So had a kissable button nose, two chubby cheeks and the
sweetest little mouth.

Love swamped her. Amber had never imagined
herself a mother, but Taylor was the greatest thing
that had ever happened to her, and looking into that
precious face, she had absolutely no choice but to
smile.

In response, Taylor let out an ear-splitting squeal
and grinned, while cheerfully, uncontrollably waving her arms.

Amber's heart twisted again and she bent, touching her nose to Taylor's. "You are the sweetest baby
that ever lived," she whispered fiercely. "I love
you."

Taylor drooled, making Amber smile again,
though her smile was bittersweet this time. Taylor
was her family, her life, her everything. They were
alone together.

And together the two of them would be just fine.

That's what Amber repeated to herself as she

strode breathlessly to the elevator and hit the button for the second floor. It didn't matter that they were unwanted—Amber by her father, Taylor by hers.

They would survive.

As she waited, she smiled at her daughter and wondered for the thousandth time if Taylor had her daddy's eyes. Were the light, crystal clear baby blues, the kind one could drown in, from Dax?

It still hurt, the not knowing. She'd tried, she reassured herself. The day after the earthquake, after she'd made the rash decision to go to Mexico for an extended vacation that had turned into a yearlong leave of absence, she'd attempted to see Dax.

In spite of her embarrassment at having to face the man she'd thrown herself at, she'd wanted to thank him for saving her life, for she held no illusions. She never would have survived without him, without his quick thinking and razor-sharp instincts, without his warm, safe arms and incredibly soothing voice.

She had no idea where he lived, but knew that as a fire inspector, he had to work out of the main fire house downtown. Somehow she'd summoned her courage to thank him in person, but when she'd gotten there, most of her bravery had faded in the face of reality.

She'd found him all right. He'd been in the break room with one of the firefighters. A woman. And they'd been laughing and teasing and flirting.

She'd prepared herself for anything, anything but

that. Standing in the doorway watching, *yearning*, she thought she'd never seen anyone so open, so absolutely full of life.

He was definitely far more man than she was equipped to handle, and with her words of thanks stuck in her throat, she'd turned tail and run. Not exactly mature, but it was done. To make up for her silliness, she'd sent a thank-you card and flowers before she'd left town.

It hadn't been until later, *much* later, that she'd discovered her condition.

Her *pregnant* condition.

The elevator doors of the medical building opened and Amber got on, straightening her shoulders and hugging Taylor close. To her credit, she had indeed again tried to reach Dax, and at *that* memory, she reddened with embarrassment.

She'd called his office from Mexico, not wanting anything from him, just needing to tell him. She figured she owed him that. He had a right to know.

He'd been in Montana, helping to fight the out-of-control range fires there. She'd left a message with an unsympathetic secretary, explaining where she was and only that she needed to talk to Dax.

He hadn't returned the call.

She understood. He'd moved on.

Yet whatever his faults, he'd once been compassionate and caring to her, and because of that, he needed to hear the truth from her own lips. In person. Though it had been easier to hide all this time, she couldn't continue it.

He had to know about Taylor.

And he would, she promised herself, now that she was back in town—just as soon as she figured out how to do it right.

The elevator doors opened and she entered a huge reception area, filled with women; young and old, sick and healthy, and very pregnant. Most had little children with them. Resigned to a long wait, Amber signed in and stood there, surveying the grumpy crowd, trying to find an empty seat. In her arms, a wide-awake Taylor shifted, stared at all the chaos around her, and let out a happy little gurgle.

"Glad someone's so cheery," Amber said with a helpless laugh. She dropped the heavy diaper bag to the floor and sighed in relief at the loss of the weight. Another grateful sigh came when she sank into an empty chair. Sitting had never felt so good.

But then, from across the room, a sea of waiting people between them, stood a man. Not just any man, but the one who could stop her heart cold.

Dax McCall.

And, oh God, he was staring right at her. *What should she do?*

All semblance of control flew out the window. So did reasoning. Sure, she could run, but even if her legs were working, running seemed so undignified. She could lie, but that was no good, either. Not only was she horrible at lying, she could never live with herself.

No, she alone had brought on this awkward situation, she would face it. Easier said than done, she thought wildly, still pierced by Dax's unwavering, highly personal stare.

For a second she allowed herself to think—hope— he wouldn't recognize her. After all, the last time he'd seen her, she'd been covered in dirt and debris, battered and afraid, and very unlike herself. And then after that, he'd not returned her call, nor acknowledged her card and flowers.

She should have known better. He recognized her.

Strangely enough, around them life went on. Babies cried, though not Taylor, who was blessedly silent. Parents chatted. Moms-to-be flipped through baby magazines. Medical staff buzzed noisily, going about their rounds and duties.

Amber saw and heard none of it, her gaze held prisoner by Dax's stare. He was exactly as he'd been in her dreams—tall, powerfully built. Unforgettable. He wore snug, faded jeans that fit his athletic physique, and a plaid flannel shirt, open and untucked over a simple white T-shirt.

Plain clothes, not such a plain man.

It didn't help that Amber could remember exactly what lay under those clothes. Though she had never actually seen him in all his naked glory, she'd *felt* him, every single inch, and what magnificent inches they had been. She knew his every muscle intimately, had personally run her hands over those broad shoulders, his wide chest, his flat stomach, those long, tough thighs...and what lay between.

In her mind she was back there, back beneath that desk, hot and panting for him. If she remembered right, and she was horribly certain she did, she'd actually begged him to take her. *Begged.*

Heat flooded her face and she was thankful he couldn't read her mind.

Still, he stood there, strong and silent. Charismatic. Even now, as he remained frozen, there were any number of women in the room shooting him frank glances of admiration.

He didn't appear to notice. In fact, he seemed to notice nothing but her.

Unsure, weak in the knees, Amber smiled feebly and was thankful she'd found a chair. The urge to fling her arms around his neck shocked her, and she decided it was some sort of delayed reaction to what they'd been through last year. After all, there'd been a time, a very brief time, when he'd been her entire world.

He moved toward her, and she held her breath. She saw the exact moment he registered what she was holding—or rather, *whom.*

Hunkering down beside her chair, he gazed with awe and wonder into Taylor's sweet face. "Yours?" he asked.

God, that voice. It should be illegal to combine that

mixture of compassion and sexuality. Her pulse beat like a drum as she nodded.

Reverently, he reached out and touched Taylor's pink blanket.

Amber closed her eyes to the sight of him, big and powerful, kneeling by his baby. *His* baby. This couldn't be happening, not like this, God, not like this. How could she still yearn for him, so much that it was a physical ache?

Her heart thundered in her chest, her blood pumping so loudly she could hardly hear herself think.

What to say? How to make this all okay?

How to make him understand?

Dammit, why hadn't she called him again? Yes, his secretary had been rude and aloof, but what if he *hadn't* received the message? How could she have been so irresponsible, just because of her own stupid fears?

"How old is she?"

"Three months. Dax…"

"At least you remembered my name." He let out a tight smile. "I wasn't sure there for a moment."

Shame heated her face, but she didn't let it show. She'd lost her control once around him. She wouldn't do it again. "I've never forgotten."

"You've obviously forgotten some of it, or you would have contacted me."

"That goes both ways."

"Do you really think I didn't try to find you?"

A thrill shot through her, and it was completely inappropriate. "I tried, too." But the feeble excuse faded at his expression. And then at his words.

"Three months," he said slowly. "You said she was three months— But that would make her... Oh my God," he said hoarsely, staring at Taylor. "Oh my God. She's mine."

The pain in his voice was real, very real, and Amber had never known such regret and grief in her life. "Dax."

"How could you not tell me?" he demanded in a hushed, serrated voice. "Did I hurt you that much? Were you that unwilling? Did you need revenge?"

"No." His hurt registered and cut like a knife to her heart. She had no idea what to do, how to make this right.

Where was her easy sophistication now, the distance she needed to pull this off? It deserted her in the face of his utterly honest reaction.

In all her life, she'd never purposely hurt another. She'd never had the power. Her father had always been impenetrable that way. Roy, her ex-fiancé, had been her father's emotional twin, or *non*-emotional. She couldn't have hurt either of them if she'd tried.

There'd been no one else, until Dax. When he hadn't returned her call, she'd figured he was much the same as the other men in her life, but she'd been wrong. Dax wasn't the cold, unfeeling sort, not at all, and she should have known. He was deeply caring and wildly passionate. She imagined he was that way about his work, his playtime, his life, everything.

He'd never hold back, never ruthlessly control himself.

She admired that. Admired it, and feared it.

He didn't move, just stood staring down at his daughter with a combination of awe and fear and devastating sorrow.

Amber couldn't help but notice that he did indeed have the same pale blue eyes as their daughter. His hair, a thick, rich brown, naturally highlighted from the sun, fell recklessly to his collar.

It was the exact shade of Taylor's.

But the physical attributes weren't important, not when compared to the heart-wrenching, awestruck way father and daughter stared at each other.

Amber's chest had tightened at the first sight of Dax, and the fist gripping her heart only tightened with each passing moment. She could hardly stand it.

"What's her name?" he demanded.

"Dax—"

"Her name, Amber."

"Taylor Anne."

"*Last* name."

Amber hesitated, only for a second, but he noticed. His jaw tightened. "It's a simple enough question, I think."

"Her last name is Riggs," she said quietly. "But you're on the birth certificate."

Dax looked at her then, with eyes as cold as ice and filled with fury.

"I have a copy of it for you," she added inanely.

"You're not going to deny it then?"

"No." Her eyes were filled with bright, scalding tears she refused to shed. "She's yours, Dax. That was the one thing I never had any doubts about."

5

"DAMN YOU," he said softly, the hardened expression on his face melting when Taylor drooled and waved two fists in the air. "How could you not have come to me?"

"I called. You weren't in your office."

He swore again, less softly and thrust his hands through his hair. "And you didn't think that maybe this deserved a second call?"

"I left a message."

Those ice-blue eyes pinned her to the spot. "I never would have pegged you as cruel, Amber. Never."

"Oh, Dax. I never meant to be, but I knew how you felt about becoming a father."

He stared at her in disbelief, so much hurt in his gaze she nearly couldn't look at him. "You know nothing about me if you thought I'd appreciate your silence on this," he said quietly.

"I'm sorry." The words were completely inadequate, and she knew it. "Dax, I'm so sorry. I knew I had to call you again. I planned to, but I just got back into town myself and…" And she'd let her fear stand in the way.

"I looked for you." His laugh was short and completely without mirth. "I wanted to see you. You were nowhere to be found."

"I went to Mexico."

"Alone?"

She nodded.

He looked away from her, down into Taylor's face. His eyes warmed and he lifted a finger to stroke it down the baby's face. "What about your family? You didn't go to them?"

Amber thought of her father, and how he'd reacted to the news of her pregnancy. After his shock, he'd recovered quickly, blaming her mother's genes. He'd told Amber she was an embarrassment to him. Worse. And that he didn't want to see her ever again.

She couldn't admit that shame to Dax. "Going to my family wasn't an option."

"No? Well coming to me should have been. You should have told me. I should have been there. For you, for Taylor. For *me*."

"I thought—"

"You had no right to make that decision for me, no matter what you thought." His voice was no more than a whisper, but it was so harsh, she cringed.

"You cheated me," he said. "You cheated *her*, your own daughter."

Amber knew that, God she knew, and she couldn't possibly feel more cruel or guilty. Speaking past the lump of emotion in her throat was impossible.

"Um...Dax?"

At the soft voice behind them, he stiffened, then drew in an agitated breath before carefully rising to his feet to face the woman who was looking at them, confused.

With clear difficulty, Dax smiled at the beautiful, tall blonde whose stomach seemed ready to pop. "You should be sitting down somewhere," he said, his voice hoarse. "Waiting for your appointment."

"What's the matter?" the woman asked, reaching out for him. "Something's wrong."

"I'm fine," he said.

"No—"

"Suzette."

Something in his voice must have warned her. Now the woman looked Amber over in frank curiosity, and Amber looked right back. She couldn't help herself.

Another pregnancy?

"I'm Suzette," the woman said to her, thrusting out her hand.

Amber stared at it, automatically lifting her own from years of enforced manners, wishing she'd stayed in Mexico, wishing that she and Dax could have had this inevitable confrontation without his "latest" witnessing it, wishing that she was anywhere but here.

"Suzette, this is Amber Riggs," Dax said.

"Oh, are you a friend of Dax?" Suzette asked her.

Amber figured that as a not-so-subtle attempt to figure out the relationship between her and Dax, and she would have liked to crawl in a hole. "Well—" She glanced at Dax.

No help at all, he just looked at her from fathomless eyes.

Fine. She could handle this. "It's been awhile since we've—"

Dax raised a brow.

"—seen each other," she finished. "A year."

"Well it must be nice to run into each other." Suzette smiled. "And here of all places. How funny."

Hysterical.

Taylor chose that moment to squeal loudly, making her instant hunger known to everyone within hearing distance. Amber tried to soothe her by giving her a pacifier, but she spit it out and turned bright red, a sure sign of an upcoming fit.

"Let me," Dax said, reaching for the baby. His eyes dared Amber to defy him.

She wouldn't, not over this. She handed Taylor over.

At the loss of her mom's arms, Taylor let out an indignant howl.

"What's the matter, sweetheart?" Dax asked, expertly cuddling the baby close.

She's had only me! Amber wanted to say, but at the equal mixture of terror and joy on Dax's face, she restrained herself. "She's hungry. I have formula."

"You aren't...?" Dax jutted his chin out toward her chest. "Breastfeeding?"

"Yes," Amber said quickly, feeling herself go red

at his bluntness. To add insult, her body betrayed her by reacting to his nonsexual gaze in a very sexual way. Her tummy fluttered, her nipples hardened. "When we're out, I'd rather give her a bottle."

"Oh." Appeased, Dax looked down at his daughter, his expression so bare and honest and fierce she could hardly stand it.

Suzette jumped when her name was called from the main desk. "Oh, dear. It's time."

"Yeah." Dax nodded toward a man who'd just gotten off the elevator. "Look, there's Alan. You'll have a ride home."

"But—"

"See you," he said, kissing her cheek, nudging her gently away.

The look Suzette shot Dax over her shoulder was filled with questions.

"Have a good one," Dax said, waving, ignoring her silent curiosity. "Talk to you later."

"Yeah. You'd better." With one last glance, Suzette left them to walk toward the man, but that last look Dax received wasn't difficult to read.

She wanted answers.

Amber wondered if she'd get them. "She's pretty," she said inanely. "When is she due?"

"A week or so."

Taylor reached out with a wet fist, and partly by luck, latched onto the front of Dax's T-shirt. There was already a drool stain down the front of him, then she tugged, wrinkling it. Amber winced but Dax simply cupped the back of her little head with his big hand and smiled at her.

Watching them, Amber's heart wrenched. She didn't want to see how wonderfully perfect the two of them looked together, father and daughter, but there was no missing it. "Shouldn't you be going into the appointment with Suzette?"

"Me?" Dax glanced after Suzette's wobbly figure. "She'll be okay."

Anger vanquished her guilt. "Oh, I see. You don't need to be there for all the hard work, right? Only the fun stuff."

Dax's mouth opened at that, then carefully shut. In spite of the hurt and anger still clearly visible, he let out a little disbelieving laugh. "Tell me you don't think Suzette's baby is *mine*."

Amber lifted her chin, gave him her best intimidation stare.

He didn't even flinch. "My God. You do."

"I don't know what I think."

"Yes, you do. You're just too polite to share it."

She lifted her chin another notch and he shook his head, disgusted. "Suzette's my sister, Amber. Alan is her husband."

It was hard to remain indignant, she realized, when she was an idiot. "Oh."

"Yeah, *oh*." He leaned close, close enough that she caught the scent of him, one hundred percent male. It was so achingly familiar, it would surely haunt her that night.

"*Fun* stuff?" he asked, his brow raised. "Is that what you call it?"

She managed to keep her eyes level with his, barely, but she couldn't control the blush she felt creeping up her face.

"I have to admit, I find it as 'fun' as the next guy," he said a little thickly, his gaze dropping to her mouth for just an instant. "But as I recall, what we shared was a hell of a lot hotter than just 'fun.' In fact, it was downright scorching."

Though he was right, she swallowed hard. The ball of lust he'd created inside her didn't go down though. "Stop it."

"You headlined my fantasies for weeks," he told her in that same sexy tone. "The way you cried my name, remember? And those sexy little mewling sounds you make when you come—"

"Stop."

The teasing left him instantly and he straightened. "You're right, this is not amusing. Not in the slightest." He shifted Taylor closer, looking like a natural dad. "Let me ease your mind," he said curtly, in direct opposition to the gentle way he surrounded his daughter. "I told you I'm not married. That's still true."

The leap in her heart was ruthlessly ignored.

"And you're right about one thing," he agreed. "I might never have *chosen* to be a father, not yet, but in no way does that mean I won't be the best dad in the world to my baby. I'm a responsible man, Amber, though I have no idea why I'm explaining myself to you, when you obviously didn't care enough to even ask."

"Dax—"

Taylor, tired of waiting, let out another warning cry. She still had a grip on Dax's shirt, and with a kick of her legs, she tugged. Dax grimaced and unsuccessfully attempted to untangle Taylor's fist. "She's got chest hair in that fist," he said, pained.

Good. But Dax's second wince reached her, and with a sigh, she stepped close. "Let me help—"

Their hands touched, his big and rough, hers small and elegant.

The connection was startlingly electric, and given the way Dax went suddenly still, he felt it, too.

They stared at each other stupidly.

Ever since the earthquake, Amber had convinced herself that their undeniable attraction was a direct result of the death threat they'd been under.

Another untruth, it seemed, because there was no threat of death here, and that almost chemical heat between them existed strong as ever.

It was easier to stand and busy herself with loosening Taylor's little fist than to meet Dax's unwavering gaze. Only problem—now she was face-to-face with him, mere inches away, touching his shirt and chest with a familiar intimacy that made thinking difficult.

"Care to share that thought?" he wondered. "The one that's making you blush?"

Her fingers faltered. "No."

"Chicken," he taunted softly.

Her lips tightened, and she might have given him a frosty comment, if she hadn't noticed his breathing wasn't any more steady than hers.

Mercifully, Taylor's name was called from the front desk.

Amber looked up at Dax. He looked right back.

"I need to take her in," she said softly, holding out her hands for the baby.

Dax didn't relinquish her. "I'm coming." His face had hardened into the stubborn expression of a man with a fight on his hands.

But she had no intention of giving him one. She didn't intend to keep Taylor from him, nor did she want to hurt him in any way.

"And then we're going somewhere to settle this," he said firmly.

At that, her good intentions faltered. Memories crowded her, unhappy ones. Always, her father's word had been law. Roy had turned out to be much the same way. All her life, she'd told herself someday things would be different, and now they were.

No one was the boss of her. Not even the man she'd had a child with. She'd share Taylor with Dax because it was the right thing to do, but she'd *never* let him run her life.

"*Settle* this?" she repeated evenly, as though her heart hadn't settled in her windpipe. Would he try to take Taylor away from her? Would he tell the courts she was an unworthy mother, just as her own mother had been? "What do you mean by that exactly?"

"I mean that this is far from over."

"Yes, but—"

"Taylor," the nurse called again, and without another word Dax turned, and still holding Taylor, headed toward the waiting nurse, leaving her to follow.

She hated that, mostly because she had never trusted anyone to lead the way for her before, and yet, that very lack of trust had led directly to the trouble she now found herself in.

BY THE TIME they got to Amber's condo, Dax's head was spinning. He had so many emotions running through his mind he was amazed he could even speak. He didn't ask, but simply followed Amber inside.

He couldn't take it all in.

He had a baby.

He was a father.

And then there was Amber herself. Her artfully cut, shiny dark hair still came only to her chin. Her even darker eyes were huge in her face, and full of haunting secrets.

But he thought she was the most attractive woman he'd ever been with. He'd always thought so, from that very first day.

Certainly his daughter was the most beautiful baby he'd ever laid eyes on. He'd held her through her doctor's appointment, staring in stunned amazement at her scrawny little limbs and rounded belly, watching enthralled at the way she screwed up her face with fury when the nurse undressed her.

She had a hell of a temper, he'd noted with some amusement, and none of her mother's cool control. No, his baby girl was all McCall, wearing everything she felt right on her sleeve for the world to see.

And she was his. *His.*

He was a father. He was a father. *Dear God, he was a father.*

Honestly, he didn't know whether to dance or cry, but could have easily done both. "Excuse me," he said, moving past a startled Amber into her living room, and folding his liquidy legs, he carefully set Taylor—still in her carrier—on the couch. He sank down next to her and just stared at her.

"Dax?"

"I'm a father, Amber."

She sighed. "Yes."

The hesitation in her answer reminded him she hadn't come to him. He'd *happened* upon her. The betrayal, even for a woman he didn't really know, cut deep. Dax wasn't perfect, not even close, but he was honest to a fault and expected others to be as well. He'd never have thought Amber capable of this.

"I want to understand," he said, still looking at his baby. "But for the life of me, I can't."

"Understand?"

"Why?" He lifted his head. "How could you not tell me?"

The question, or maybe his face, had her unbuckling Taylor and pulling her into her arms, possessively, protectively, so much so that it was painful to witness.

She actually looked hurt, afraid...and he didn't understand.

He was the wronged party here!

"The reasons don't seem to make much sense now," she admitted, kissing the top of Taylor's head.

"Try me."

"All right." She was in control now, her voice smooth, her gaze steady. "What we had was a fling, Dax. Neither of us wanted more, or would have wanted to drag it out."

Why that infuriated him, he couldn't have said. Maybe because he'd so foolishly looked for her afterward. And then ached for so long at her disappearance. "Speak for yourself."

Her gaze floundered but she remained outwardly calm. "All right. Long after it was over, and a full month into my vacation—"

"Vacation. Don't you mean your Leave-From-Life?"

"—I discovered I was pregnant," she finished without looking at him. "I tried to contact you. You didn't call me back."

"I didn't get your message."

"I'm sorry. I knew I had to try again, but I..." Her

jaw tightened. "There are no excuses really. I was wrong. I'm sorry for that, so very sorry." Something haunting flickered across her face. "I was used to being alone, so it seemed rational to do this alone, too."

Dammit, he absolutely didn't want to see that flash of vulnerability, didn't want to be touched by it. With all his being he needed to hold onto his anger. "You're going to have to get over that," he said, not very kindly. "Being alone."

She said nothing to that, and since she was the queen bee at hiding her emotions, he had no idea what she was thinking. She settled Taylor in a playpen, where the baby stared happily up at a musical mobile, kicking excitedly.

Dax could have watched that little girl all day long, but at the moment, the show was Amber. Her actions were smooth, and so purposely relaxed that he knew she had to be the exact opposite—strung tight as a drum.

"I like to be alone," she said.

"That's too bad."

She flinched.

And that was where more unwanted conflicting emotions came into play for Dax. He didn't pretend to understand this woman who had tipped his world on its axis, but at the time, he found he couldn't purposely hurt her. "I'm not threatening you," he said gruffly, hating that she clearly thought he was. "You're the mother of my child." Which made his stomach twist. "We need to talk this out, Amber."

"I know." No nervous fluttering for this woman. Standing directly in front of him, her body and hands still, her face guarded, she waited.

Waited for what exactly, he hadn't a clue. Her eyes gave nothing away, but he could have sworn she was expecting him to light into her one way or another. Again, he was struck by her cool beauty. That he knew exactly how much heat and passion lay just beneath that surface didn't help things. "Will you sit?"

"Don't."

"Don't what?"

She didn't move a muscle. "I can't handle the small talk. Just get down to it. You're going to fight me for custody."

It took him a full moment. *"What?"*

"You're going to try to take her away from me, right?"

He stared at her, shocked. She was standing there, cool as a cucumber, waiting for the ax to fall, waiting for him to try to destroy her. "Hold on." He shook his head, trying to clear it. Then he slowly stood to make them even. "Have I at any time in these past few hours said anything, *anything at all*, that could have possibly made you believe I would take Taylor from you?"

"You have to admit, it's something a person in your position would consider."

A headache started, right between his eyes. A tension headache, he realized with surprise. He almost never got tension headaches. "You've been in business too long," he said wearily. "You think with that cutthroat mentality."

She still just waited, making him sigh. Was she really cold? Or was she dying of fear inside? "I have no intention of suing you."

"But?" Her lips curved, but the smile wasn't warm. "I think I hear one at the end of that sentence."

He let out a disparaging sound and massaged his temples. "But...hell, I don't know. I can't believe I'm here, doing this." Restless, he strode to the playpen.

Taylor turned her attention from the mobile, staring at him with the somberness of an old woman. Bending closer, he smiled at her and suddenly she came to life, wiggling, waving her arms, pumping her little legs for all she was worth, cooing and babbling, doing everything in her three-month-old power to entice him to pick her up.

As if he could have resisted. He scooped her to him, cuddled her close and...nearly passed out. *"Holy smokes."* He wrinkled his nose and held her out at arm's length.

"I need to change her."

"Yeah." But at the dare he found in Amber's eyes, he held onto his stinky daughter. "I can do it." He tucked her close despite the smell and vowed not to inhale. Taylor's head bobbed, not quite steady, and he settled a hand behind her neck, supporting her.

She blinked and a long line of drool dripped from her mouth to his shoulder.

Then she gave him a toothless smile.

His heart tightened, and just like that, he fell in love.

Then she opened her mouth and spit up, hitting him full in the chest with a white, foul-smelling liquid that rivaled the scent coming from her diaper.

Amber bit her lip, and he knew damn well it was to hide her laugh. "Would you like some help?" she asked sweetly.

He had no intention of backing off now, even if his eyes were watering. "I can do this."

Obviously pleased with herself, Taylor cooed and smiled wetly.

Dax held his breath and hugged her close. He'd throw his shirt away later. "Let's go, Squirt."

TWO MINUTES into it, Dax was no longer so certain he could handle this fatherhood thing at all. He had ten nieces and nephews, and somehow he'd managed to avoid changing any of them.

Taylor lay flat on her changing table, naked and shiny clean from the sponge bath he'd given her. But for the life of him, he couldn't figure out how to get her to hold still long enough to get the diaper on her. She seemed to have twenty arms and legs, and all of them were doing the bicycle thing at the moment.

Amber appeared in the doorway, an unreadable expression on her face.

Dax wanted to think that the flash of emotion he saw was guilt, regret, sorrow, pick one of the above, but he couldn't be sure.

"Need some help?" she asked.

Yes. "I've got it." He managed to slide the diaper under Taylor's bare tush, only to have her wriggle to her side and kick it free.

"She's a slippery thing," Amber said. "Tenacious, too."

Pride filled him, and before he could remember how furious he still was, he grinned. "Yeah." Once again he tried to corral her on her back. Taylor grunted and fought him, smiling as she did.

God, she was his. *His.*

All his life he'd been a goof-off, the class clown. And all his life he'd been treated that way. He had to face the fact he'd done his best to live up to that reputation. With older sisters constantly babying him, and women frequently offering themselves, he'd never really thought of himself as particularly...well, family worthy.

Even his job, as serious and important as it was, was really just an extended form of play. He caught bad guys who started fires.

The truth was, he'd never grown up.

The realization wasn't something to be proud of, and suddenly he didn't like his image. He wanted more.

Taylor blew him a bubble.

Putty in her hands, he had to smile, thinking that maybe, just maybe, he'd just been given more.

Oh, he was still hurt at Amber's deception. Angry, too, and a whole bunch of other things he couldn't name at the moment. But he found he could deal with that separately. He wanted this child with all his heart, and he had no intention of letting anything between him and Amber stand in the way of that.

Behind him, he heard Amber shift as she came forward. He could feel her, could feel that unnamed thing that shimmered between them. Glancing at her, he found her watching him as well.

And for a long moment all that was between them disappeared. He remembered the day they'd spent locked in each other's arms. The heat, the passion, the fear, the need. It had been incredible, and he had to admit, he wouldn't have changed a thing that happened.

Except for maybe Amber's disappearance afterward.

Then he remembered, he was standing there, holding his daughter—his *daughter!*—and that Amber had kept her from him.

And just like that, the moment was gone.

With a strange sense of regret, Dax turned back to the baby and Amber left him alone, without a clue as to what she was thinking.

Nothing new.

Taylor blew him a bubble, and Dax had to let out a

laugh. "I don't think she's nearly as charmed with me as you are, sweetheart."

Taylor just drooled.

TAYLOR SLEPT peacefully, oblivious to the tension around her, her little butt sticking straight up in the air, her fist stuffed in her mouth.

Dax watched her, actually feeling his heart contract. Just looking at her hurt.

It hurt to look at her mother too, he discovered, as he came down the stairs and met Amber's deep, dark, impenetrable gaze.

"Let's get this over with," she said calmly, only her eyes giving away her nerves. "What do you want?"

"Want?" He laughed incredulously. "That's an interesting question."

"Do you have an answer?"

"How about you marry me?"

Her composure slipped on that one, but she regained it quickly enough. "Don't be ridiculous."

"Yes or no, Amber."

"It's simply not possible."

"Sure it is. You just say, 'I do.'"

She stared at him, and incredibly, he found himself wishing she'd come to him months ago. He would have been so thrilled to see her. He would have drawn her close for a hug and probably never let her go.

But marriage? His stomach cramped at the

thought. Yet how else to resolve this? He hated the thought of Taylor feeling illegitimate. Hated the thought of being separated from her after he'd just discovered her. "If we were married, then neither of us would have to be away from Taylor. Seems logical to me."

She gave a short, amazed laugh. "Logical."

"More than the alternative anyway. I just found out I have a daughter, Amber. I can't turn my back on her. Or, for some reason, you."

"I'm not an obligation."

"No," he said softly, thinking of the life-altering experience they'd shared. "You're not."

"Dax..."

Again, that thing shimmered between them. Heat. Passion. Need. But it annoyed him, and if he was truthful, it also scared him. "Look, it's simple. Yes or no."

"You're serious," she breathed, then she shook her head. "No." Her shoulders straightened. "I won't marry for anything less than..." She looked down at her hands, which were tightly clenched. She opened them, let them fall to her sides. "I am not going to marry a stranger."

"We stopped being strangers the day of the quake, when we spent hours in each other's arms, terrified, waiting to die."

"I don't usually act like that. I never act like that."

Dax thought it was a shame, but she didn't relent and he let out a sound of frustration. "Look, we're parents. Together. We *can't* be strangers, even if we wanted to be."

"The answer is still no."

"Fine. You don't want to get married." He wouldn't admit his disappointment because he couldn't believe he felt it in the first place. But neither could he ignore the feeling that, despite her calm control, she was frightened of him.

Much as he wanted to hold onto his anger and resentment, it was hard in the face of that.

"I intend to be a father. A good one. I want my daughter. Just as you do. We're adults. We can share."

She nearly sagged with what could only be described as profound relief. "You want to *share* her?"

For some reason that made him mad all over again. Dammit, he wasn't the one who should have to prove his trustworthiness! "Hell, yes, I want to share."

"You're not going to fight for custody?"

"Do I need to?"

His tightly spoken words stabbed through Amber. He stood there looking so certain, so fierce. She hadn't expected this, hadn't expected him to actually want Taylor as much as she did.

But she'd been in business a long time, and what she hadn't learned there, she'd learned from her father. Bottom line, she knew how to win a deal. Start out asking for the moon. Take all if you can. Settle for less only if you have to. "I want Taylor with me."

"Sure." He nodded agreeably. Even sent her a smile that could steal the breath from a nun. "Half the time."

Her stomach twisted. "But—"

"Stop," he said firmly, in that voice of rough velvet. Closing the distance between them, he touched her arms, slid his big, warm hands over her skin. Immediately, heat flooded her. Her body remembered his touch vividly, had craved it nearly every night since that time she'd first experienced it. The sensation of being this close to him again was so overpowering, she had to close her eyes for a moment, or reveal everything she felt.

"Look at me."

Shocked at the command, she did.

"I understand you think we're strangers," he said. "And there's a real fear in that. I'm not going to kid you. This isn't going to be easy, we're going to have to work hard. Together."

Amber tried not to panic at the thought of what getting to know him would entail. Intimacy—and she wasn't thinking of sex, but the other aspects—all of which terrified her.

With surprising gentleness, he slid his fingers up and down her arms. "I have the feeling you think I'm out to hurt you, or trick you. I'm not into games, Amber. You've been hurt before, maybe so much so that you feel you can't trust me...." He paused, studying her when she was unable to maintain eye contact.

"I see," he said quietly. He spoke huskily, as if he

cared, and it hurt to hear it because she knew all too well how little she deserved his kindness.

"I'm not like him," he told her, his hands still on her. "The ex-fiancé, or whoever hurt you."

He remembered. She couldn't believe he remembered so much about her.

"I'm not trying to frighten you, or threaten. I'm not going to bully you. But Amber—" He lifted her chin. "That baby is mine, and I plan on being a damn good father. We can do this and make it work. Together. It would be good. But it's *together*. That's the key."

God, that voice. It brought her back to the terrifying magical time she spent with him, a time she could never forget because she'd felt so safe and warm and...wanted.

Unbelievably, she felt wanted now.

"It has to have been hard to do this all alone," he murmured. "She's a little handful. You must be exhausted. Wouldn't some help be nice? From someone with as big a stake as you?"

Amber felt a tiny seed of long-dead hope take root. Was it possible he could forgive her? That maybe he could want *her* as much as he wanted Taylor? That he could grow to love and care for her as well as Taylor, the *real* her, the way no one else ever had?

She allowed herself to think about it. To consider it. To dream.

"We'll make up a schedule," he said, dropping his

hands and stepping back. "That's the easiest way, unless you have a better idea."

"A schedule?"

"It's the civil servant in me." He flashed a surprisingly self-deprecating smile. "I like routine."

"I don't understand."

"To divide Taylor between us so there's no problem."

"Divide her," she repeated inanely, her stomach dropping to the ground.

"I don't plan on being a weekend dad, Amber. I'm willing to share, but we do it equally."

Well what did she expect? She'd turned down his marriage proposal. But still, the hope within her died a cruel death. He wanted Taylor, not her mother. Amber lifted her chin, because no matter what he said, she could depend on no one, no one but herself. "Fine. We share."

"Equally."

Oh, God. She was actually going to have to do this, give him Taylor. Her eyes burned, threatened to flood. "I said fine."

"Good."

She needed him gone. "You can start tomorrow. Bring your schedule if you must, but for now, for today, she's mine alone. I don't want to share my day."

Dammit, he looked hurt again. "It doesn't have to be so cut-and-dried."

"Yes, it does."

"Why?"

Because she knew nothing else. "All we're sharing is Taylor. There's nothing else to worry about. Absolutely nothing."

"Are you talking about our attraction?"

"There is no attraction. None. None at all."

His eyes narrowed. "Who are you trying to convince?"

"I'm already convinced."

He took a step toward her and she fought against instinct and stood still.

"So you look at me and feel nothing?" he wondered aloud.

When he took another step, she nearly bolted. Sheer willpower held her there. "That's right."

"You don't remember what happened between us? Hell, what *exploded* between us?"

"This isn't about us—" she stuttered silent when he touched her. "And it's sure not about sex."

"Oh, yes, it is." His voice had lowered, which for some reason made her tummy tingle, but she could ignore that. What she couldn't ignore was the look in his eyes, the lingering hurt mixed in with a good amount of pride and scorching intensity.

"It's not about what *I* feel," she insisted. "Besides, you can't possibly feel something for me, after what I've done." Her voice was a mere whisper as renewed shame crept up her spine. "I kept her from you, remember?"

"I remember." He touched her face and her eyes

nearly closed in pleasure. "You still have to tell me you feel nothing for me," he reminded her.

"I—" She hesitated and saw his eyes flare with triumph. "I don't have to tell you anything." She stood back and crossed her arms over her chest. "Goodbye, Dax."

He stared at her. After a moment, he shook his head and went to the door. "I'll come for Taylor in the morning."

He was leaving. She'd chased him away. Relief, she should feel relief.

She didn't.

And then she was alone, again. Always alone.

6

THEY SETTLED into a pattern, splitting Taylor between the two of them. Dax would have her on Tuesdays and Thursdays, and every other weekend.

It might have been a perfect arrangement, for any other man.

But as a week passed, and then another, Dax realized it wasn't enough, it would never be enough. He wanted more, he wanted it all.

How did other single fathers do it, share their children with their exes? He didn't know.

Even worse, he actually found himself forgiving Amber. Or if not forgiving completely, at least understanding her. He didn't like it.

Thanks to the luck of his schedule, he'd managed to work only on the days Amber had Taylor. But two weeks after he learned he had a daughter, both work and the baby came on the same day.

It was an experience, to say the least. His family had fallen in love with Taylor, and any of them would have dropped everything to baby-sit, but he wasn't ready to give her up yet.

So baby in tow, he went to his office, confident he could handle it.

Taylor started out the workday fast asleep in her carrier, and everything seemed great. The guys in his office kept poking their heads in to coo over her and Dax kept shooing them out so they wouldn't wake her. But when Taylor's morning nap was over, so was his day.

She cried while he was on the phone to the mayor. She threw up on one of his investigative reports. Then her diaper leaked all over his shirt, causing people to wrinkle their noses when they came too close to him. After a noisy fit over having to drink a bottle with a nipple that infuriated her, Taylor finally, *finally*, blessedly fell back asleep.

By that time, Dax was so exhausted, he fell asleep, too, face down on his desk.

And awoke to his daughter's cries. Picking her up, he pressed her close and expected her to stop crying, as she always did.

No go. In fact, she worked herself up to a furious red, screaming, mass of rage. Dax tried everything; singing like an idiot, dancing like a bigger idiot, and finally begging. Nothing worked, though it amused the staff members who gathered in his doorway to watch.

Taylor was having none of it. Finally, when her screams threatened to bring down the house, he called Amber.

"I've done something to her," he said over Taylor's howl. "I—"

"I'll be right there."

Dax paced while he waited, holding a sobbing Taylor. When Amber finally appeared, he could have kissed her. "What have I done to her?"

Amber shook her head and took the baby.

Immediately, the baby hiccuped and stopped crying.

The silence was deafening.

Amber continued to sooth her with a wordless murmur, patting her gently on the back. While Dax stared in amazement, Taylor started making loud, smacking noises with her lips, her little hands fisted in Amber's blouse.

She sounded like a starving kitten.

"She can't be hungry," he said in disbelief. "I gave her a bottle. She refused to even look at it."

"Well..." Amber looked everywhere but at him. "The bottle isn't what she wants."

"She doesn't want— Oh. *Oh,*" he said, understanding finally dawning. "She wants breast milk." He laughed, the relief so overwhelming he could hardly stand. "But she's taken formula from me before."

"I told you, she's a bit fickle."

He grinned, now that he could breathe again. "Stubborn as hell, you mean. Gee, I guess she got that from both sides, huh? Here..." Leading Amber to a chair, he backed up a few steps and waited for her to satisfy his obviously starving daughter.

Amber just looked at him.

Taylor, frustrated, turned even redder in the face and let loose with her piercing cries.

"Hurry!" Lord, how could such a small, adorable bundle of baby make so much noise? "Damn, she's got a set of lungs on her."

Amber undid her blouse, then hesitated.

Dax had been staring at Taylor's mottled face, but when Amber didn't make a move, he lifted his gaze.

It caught on the strip of creamy skin she'd revealed from throat to belly. Just like that, his body temperature rose ten degrees.

"I can't do this while you watch, Dax."

It didn't matter if she breast-fed in front of him. Not when he had a good imagination, and it was off and racing now. It didn't take much to picture her peeling the material away from her flesh, exposing one softly rounded breast. The nipple would pucker and tighten, and when Taylor pulled her mouth away, the tip would be wet and swollen.

At the thought, he went weak in the knees. Disgusted with himself, he turned and left the office, going in search of a glass of very cold water.

A cold shower might have been more effective.

No matter how much he didn't want to have feelings for this woman who'd ripped him apart, he did, and that confused him. He wasn't used to being confused where women were concerned.

He could tell himself that this deep attraction was due to Taylor, but that would be a big, fat lie. Already he loved Taylor with all his heart.

But Amber was a separate deal entirely. He'd forgiven her, yes. But he didn't want to forget.

THE NEXT TIME Amber came to the station to pick up the baby, her face was drawn. She was even more quiet and guarded than usual. She offered Dax one unreadable glance and went directly to Taylor, who was lying on a blanket and happily chewing on her own sleeve.

"Hey, baby," she whispered, her face lighting up with the smile Dax had never, not once, seen directed at him.

Taylor wriggled with joy.

"Well, you lived through it," Amber said to Dax over her shoulder.

"What about Taylor?"

"I wasn't concerned." She paused. "You're a good father."

"A compliment, Amber?"

Her spine stiffened. "No, just fact. Taylor can be a lot of work."

"You're not saying my daughter is a handful, are you?"

Amber turned and looked at him, lifting a brow at his teasing tone. Her gaze swept his office, taking in the full wastebasket, the sagging diaper bag, the baby paraphernalia scattered around the room.

And in the corner, at Amber's feet, was the happily babbling, little handful herself.

In her well-fitted power suit, Amber kneeled on

the floor and tickled Taylor's tummy. "So how was it, sweetie? Did you have a good time?"

Taylor responded with a big grin and some drool.

"Should have seen her," Dax told her. "She was in high form today. Spit up on the fire chief."

Amber's smile widened as she watched Taylor. "Did you torture your daddy today, sweetie? Did you? Tell me you did."

What tortured Dax now was Amber herself. She wasn't a tall woman, but she had legs to die for. And with her bent over as she was, he got quite an eyeful, up to midthigh. He wondered if those sheer, silky looking stockings ended at the top of those incredible legs, like the ones she'd been wearing on the day of the earthquake.

Oblivious, Amber leaned even closer to Taylor, nuzzling at the baby's neck. Taylor squealed in delight.

Dax swallowed hard, because while he'd felt every inch of Amber's body that fateful day so long ago, he'd never really *seen* her, and he'd certainly never gotten such a great view of the most mouth-watering, perfectly rounded rear end in town.

"She looks good," Amber said of the baby.

"So do you." The words popped out before he could stop them, but even when Amber whirled in shock and stared at him, he smiled, refusing to take them back.

"That was...inappropriate," she said primly.

"No doubt. It was also the truth."

As if realizing the suggestiveness of her position, she got up carefully, managing to keep her skirt from rising any further. No ungraceful scrambling for this woman, nope she remained cool as ice.

"You were looking at me."

The words were spoken evenly, yet with such surprise, Dax had to laugh. "And is that so hard to believe?"

"Men don't usually look at me that way." She glanced away. "Never, actually."

Odd how she could appear so strong, yet so utterly vulnerable at the same time. "Then they're blind. You're beautiful, Amber."

She searched his gaze, clearly wondering if he was still teasing her.

"Just looking at you makes me think of hot kisses and stolen touches."

She blushed. *Blushed.* So, the cool woman *could* be shaken. "Oh, I'm sorry," he said, anything but. "I'm being inappropriate again, aren't I?"

"You know you are." Tough facade back in place, she walked the room, passed the piles of work on his desk, passed the additional piles that had simply overflowed to the floor. He'd vacuumed before setting Taylor down, so the vacuum cleaner was still in the corner. His coat, which had fallen from the rack, lay crumpled in a heap. His boots were sprawled on the floor, discarded after his last inspection. So was the bag his lunch had come in, from his favorite hamburger joint.

"You're a pig," she said lightly, scooping up his jacket and placing it on a hook.

He wondered at the gesture. Was it because she cared, or because she cared that Taylor was in such a messy room? "Talk to your daughter. She's been a busy girl today."

A small smile crossed her lips. But Dax could see past the exterior, past that cool defense she wore like a coat. Deep in thought, he stared at her.

"What?" she asked when he came close. She didn't fidget like normal women, so she didn't pat her hair or look herself over for flaws. But her eyes chilled in response to his silent study. "What are you staring at?"

Dax knew how to soothe a woman, but he had the feeling the usual compliments and flirtations wouldn't work with Amber. She was different. Very different. Her dark, gorgeous eyes looked bruised, rimmed with light purple. Her mouth, carefully painted, was tight, pinched. And those shoulders, the ones that seemed to be strong enough to carry the burdens of the entire world, were strained, as if the weight had become too heavy.

"Stop looking at me like that," she demanded.

"Like what?"

"Like...you're hungry, or something."

Oh yeah, he was hungry. For her. How long, he wondered, would it take a man to dig under those walls? To find the real Amber, the one who'd had the guts to have a child by herself, the one he knew would protect that child with everything she had?

"Why are you *still* staring at me?"

Because she looked exhausted. Because she was a puzzle he couldn't put together. Because he couldn't seem to help himself. Backing her to a chair, he applied pressure on her arm until she sat.

"I don't have time to sit." Her voice was weary. "I still have to run to the grocery store, pick up the dry-cleaning and then when I get home, I have a report—" Carefully, she closed her mouth and in a rare gesture of emotion, ran her hands over her eyes. "I have no idea why I'm telling you all of this."

"Because you're too tired. If you weren't, you wouldn't say a word, you'd handle it all. Alone, most likely. But we're a unit now, Amber. You should be able to vent."

"And that means you'll vent, too, I suppose."

"If I need to, yes."

She looked so genuinely unsettled that he wondered what her definition of vent was. "How about I keep Taylor while you do your errands? She's fine here, the guys come in every two seconds just to look at her anyway. She'll be entertained. I'll bring her home to you later."

"I can't take advantage that way."

"Amber." He came from a family of touchers. It seemed perfectly natural for him to lift a hand and touch her cheek. And if he enjoyed the feel of her soft skin so much that he left his fingers there for an in-

stant longer than he'd planned, what did it matter?
He was just trying to comfort.

Okay, maybe it was more complicated than that,
but he wasn't ready to go there.

And besides, she backed away.

"Why do you do that?" he wondered. "Shy away
from touch?"

"I don't like to be touched."

"You did once."

A delicious shade of red colored her face. "I
should make it clear to you," she said in that prim
voice he was perversely beginning to enjoy. "I'm not
being coy here. I acted...wild with you then. I'm not
going to do it again."

"Are you thinking wild is a bad thing?"

She looked at him steadily.

"Or that I don't respect you?"

Still, just that look. Damn, she brought new meaning to the word stubborn. "What happened between
us was spontaneous, yes," he agreed. "Hot, most definitely. Even wild. But Amber, it was as necessary at
that moment as breathing, you have to remember
that much."

"It wasn't necessary."

He'd have liked to prove her wrong, right there on
the floor of his office. He had no doubt he could do it.
She had passion and heat simmering just beneath
her surface, all he had to do was set fire to it. The way
they kissed, it should only take two seconds.

But he wouldn't, because he didn't like how easily

he'd come to forgive her, and he sure as hell didn't like the way he yearned for her, even now. "Even before I knew about Taylor, I wanted to see you again."

"Of course you did. I slept with you after only knowing you an hour."

"Are you talking about when we made love?"

"Sex," she said calmly enough, but the words came out her teeth. "We had sex."

"That's not how I remember it." He smiled wickedly, figuring her imagination could taunt her with exactly what he was remembering. It would serve her right, since he'd been doing nothing *but* remembering.

"I acted cheaply. I don't like thinking about it."

"Cheap?" he asked incredulously, oddly hurt. "That's the *last* thing that comes to my mind when I think of that day." She turned away but he took her arms, forcing her to look at him. "God, Amber, we were terrified. We thought we were going to die. We needed to feel hope. We needed to feel alive, and we did, in each other's arms. How could you have forgotten all that?"

She might have pushed away, but he held her still. "No, listen to me." Somehow it had become critical to him that she not regret what they'd shared. "You didn't betray yourself that day, it just happened. And it was...right. *Very* right, dammit."

Her tortured look faded somewhat. "It gave me Taylor," she said quietly.

"It gave *us* Taylor," he corrected. "And I'll never forget it."

They stared at each other, so close that he could have leaned forward a fraction and kissed her soft, very kissable lips, but he didn't. Much as his body ached for hers, she'd burned him before, and he wasn't interested in getting burned again. "And as for tonight. You're not taking advantage, I offered. I'll even bring dinner."

"Why?"

"You know, all that mistrust is getting really old."

"I'm not mistrustful."

He laughed. "Granted, it's well hidden behind that sophisticated, sleek business front, but it's there."

"Why are you bringing me dinner?"

"See? Right there. Mistrust."

She rolled her eyes.

"I'm bringing dinner because I'll be hungry."

"Oh." She thought about it and started to give him a suspicious look, which she quickly squelched. "I suppose that would be all right."

"Good." He'd have shown up whether she liked it or not. If he knew his little daughter, and he was beginning to know her quite well, he figured Amber hadn't had a hot meal or a decent night's sleep in over three months. That was going to change.

"Go on," he said, pulling her up, nudging her to the door. "We'll see you later." Then he ushered her out before she could gather her wits to resist, which he knew she would have done if she hadn't been dead on her feet.

When she was gone, Dax turned to Taylor, hands on hips, a mock frown on his face. "You've been tiring out your parents," he said, picking her up and holding her close.

Taylor gummed a wet smile.

"It's got to stop. You hear me?"

She let out a sweet little giggle.

Dax kissed her noisily, making her wriggle with delight, which in turn warmed his heart in ways he'd never imagined.

He couldn't fathom being without her.

He was beginning to understand he felt the same way about her mother.

DAX ARRIVED at Amber's condo at exactly 7:07 p.m. with Taylor in one arm and dinner in the other. Not that Amber had been pacing, watching the clock for the past hour and a half.

She reached for Taylor and squeezed her so tight the baby mewled in protest. Amber couldn't help herself; she'd missed Taylor so much. She kissed the baby's nose and then her face, and then nearly leaped out of her skin at the sexy, unbearably familiar voice behind her.

"I'll take one of those."

Slowly, she turned. "You'll take one of what?"

"A kiss."

Her tummy fluttered. "Hmph."

He grinned, and the butterflies in her stomach took wing. What was it about him? He should have hated her. Or at the very least, still been furious. That he wasn't, and that he looked at her in a way that both confused her and made her...hot, was greatly disturbing.

"Hungry?" he asked, lifting a bag from a local deli.

"It's my father's birthday," she said slowly, her mouth watering at the smell coming from the brown bag. "I was going to call him."

"Call him. See if he'll join us."

He wouldn't, Amber knew that. But she found she couldn't admit any such thing to Dax. So, as he watched her with that quiet intensity of his, she picked up the phone and dialed the number.

"Hello, Dad," she said calmly when her father answered, as if her heart hadn't leaped into her throat at the sound of his voice after so long. "I wanted to wish you happy birthday."

Her voice was steady. Steady was important, even if she was so nervous she felt as though she might shatter at any moment. "I was also hoping you'd come for dinner and meet your granddaughter."

"Not likely," came the voice that had ruled her childhood. "Not when her mother is a slut."

Dax moved closer, but she held the phone tight to her ear so he couldn't hear. "I'm sorry you're still upset with me, but there's no need for it." She hesitated, then said softly, "I'm not like Mom. Really, I'm not."

"Did you marry that baby's father?"

"M-marry?" She glanced at Dax over her shoulder and found him still looking right at her. "Uh...no." With a carefully blank face, she pointed to the living room, gesturing him away. Anywhere, as long as he was far from her and this conversation.

Dax just settled back and lifted a brow.

With a sound of impatience, Amber covered the phone. "Go," she whispered.

"Maybe *I* should have extended the invite," he murmured. And then he grabbed the phone right out of her hands.

"Give that back!"

"Not yet." He held the phone out of her reach before bringing the receiver to his ear. He had to use his other hand to hold Amber off, but he did so with no problem, slipping one strong, warm arm around her. His forearm banded across her back, his fingers came to just above her rib cage, holding her stronger than a vise.

All she could think was that his fingers were pressed against the curve of her breast. Unbelievably, because she hated being restrained, her nipples tightened. Her breath quickened.

As if he could tell, Dax looked down into her face, his own breath coming a little faster.

"Give me the phone, Dax," she murmured.

His fingers spread wide and brushed the underside of her left breast.

She melted a little. "*Now*."

He shook his head. "Hello," he said politely into the phone, his fingers driving her to distraction. "I'm Daxton McCall, Taylor's father."

Amber groaned. Her father had never approved of her, and this wasn't going to help. He was convinced she led a wild, out-of-control lifestyle, and very likely, this conversation would confirm it.

She shouldn't care that she disappointed him, but she did, and still, to this day, wished she could make everything right, wished that her father missed his own flesh and blood the way she missed having a family.

"I'm taking full responsibility for Taylor," Dax said into the phone. "Any questions?" He continued to smile in that easygoing manner as he ruined her life, but Amber could see there was steel lining that smile and he was not kidding around. Dax was deadly serious and more than a little dangerous looking.

"We'd love you to join us tonight," he said. "Oh, you can't? Then how about you and I meet tomorrow, for lunch. I'm in the inspection office, downtown fire station. Yes. You can express all your anger and disappointment, and you can do it with me. Not Amber. Okay? See you then."

Amber gaped at him as he hung up.

"I hate bullies," he said conversationally.

Too late, Amber remembered she didn't gape as a rule. It was, however, much more of a struggle to control herself than usual. She was discovering that was the norm with Dax. "I can't believe he wants to meet you."

"Well he really wants to punch me in the nose, but he'll settle for a good look at me. I'm going to give it to him."

"He was…nice?"

"Let's say he was polite." He smiled. "Definitely curious."

In less than two minutes Dax had gotten the approval from her father that she'd been fighting for all her life.

It was deflating, depressing and demoralizing, not to mention infuriating.

"Amber?"

She was perfectly aware that her fury was illogical, that she was about to direct it toward the wrong person, but she couldn't help herself. "I want you to go now."

"What?" He looked so stunned she nearly laughed, but this wasn't a laughing matter. *"Why?"*

"I realize you probably don't get a lot of rejections. Consider this a learning experience."

"Amber, listen to me." He took her shoulders in his big hands to see that she did just that. "I can see that you care what he thinks—"

"I don't."

"Of course you do, it's natural." His understanding and compassion were far more than she could take at the moment, but he wouldn't let her move away from him. "I don't want to cause you any grief.

That's why I'm going to meet him, to take some of the pressure off of you."

Couldn't he see that just having him in her life was causing grief? Couldn't he see that she needed him to leave, now, before she did something really stupid? Like crying on his broad, capable, oh-so-comfy shoulder? She was alone in this. She *wanted* to be alone in this. "I'm really tired."

"Oh, baby, I know that one." His smile was warm, sweet, caring. And when he slid his fingers over her cheek as if she was the most important person in his world, her throat burned.

"Why are you doing this? Being nice?"

"Because..." He lifted a shoulder. "It's better than harboring resentment. It feels good. Because I want to. Pick one."

"But—"

"Amber, don't you ever get tired of fighting it?"

"It?"

"It." He stroked her jaw with his thumb, then touched the racing pulse at the base of her throat. "This."

"I...don't know what you're talking about."

His gaze took a leisurely sweep over her body, ending at the straining button between her breasts. On either side, her hard, aching nipples pressed against the material of her blouse. He seemed fascinated by the play of his fingers over her collarbone. "Don't you?" he murmured. "Don't deny it, I can see that you do."

With a huff of vexation, she crossed her arms. "I can't help that."

"I'm glad." His smoldering eyes met hers now. "I'm glad you can't control the attraction between the two of us, it's the only way I know I'm reaching you at all."

To hell with control and finesse. To hell with appearances. Screw all of it, she needed him gone, now, before she made a complete fool of herself and tore her clothes off, and then his. She marched to the front door and opened it. "Good night, Dax."

He frowned, though whether at her husky voice or her abruptness, she didn't know.

"Look, it's nothing personal," she assured him. "It's just that I've had enough of men running my life, manipulating me, and deciding what's right for me."

He went very still. "And you think that's what I'm doing?"

"Aren't you? You want me to share Taylor—"

"She's mine, too, Amber. Get it through that pretty, thick head of yours." He cupped her face in his hands, tipping it up to meet his intense gaze. His fingers on her skin made her knees knock together. So did looking at his lips and she wondered, totally inappropriately, if he kissed her now, would she melt as she had a year ago?

Probably.

Definitely.

Which was another reason to get him out of here,

quickly. But he wasn't budging, his big body was a stubborn brick wall she couldn't move.

"I hate it that you shy away from me, from the connection between us," he said.

She swallowed at the real glimpse of pain she saw in his eyes. Dammit, did he have to be so sensitive, so open and warm, so...perfect? "I don't feel any particular connection."

He set his hand to the base of her throat, let his fingers once again slide against the skin where her pulse beat wildly. "Liar," he chided softly.

"Good night, Dax."

He stared at her for one long moment, then walked to the door.

A small voice inside her head told her he was right. She *was* a liar. She *wanted* him to stay, *wanted* him to seduce her.

Or maybe *she'd* seduce *him*. It was mortifying to realize how close she was to letting her hormones run her, just as her mother had.

"You'll dream of me," he said.

She had a feeling he was right, but she shut the door and bolted it. Then she stood there for a moment, touching the door as if it were him.

Her body sizzled. *Sizzled.* A mother wasn't supposed to sizzle! She didn't want this. It would never work, not under these circumstances, not under the *best* of circumstances. Still, she nearly whipped the front door open again.

Instead, she went into the kitchen and ate as if she

was still pregnant, refusing to feel guilty for eating a good portion of Dax's food, too.

Later, after she took care of Taylor, she went to bed and tried to forget how fiercely Dax had defended her to her father. Tried to forget how good it had felt, for that one little second, to depend on someone other than herself.

And damn him, just like he'd said, she dreamed of him.

7

AMBER WOKE UP rumpled, still exhausted and haunted by visions of a starving Dax.

In the light of day she had to laugh at herself. So she'd eaten his dinner. He was a pretty capable guy, certainly he'd managed.

She got out of bed and checked on Taylor, who was still fast asleep. Grateful, she took the baby monitor and headed for the shower. Afterward, warm and steamy and still wet, she caught a glimpse of herself in the mirror. It was rare to spend any time really looking at herself, especially naked, but she looked now.

Somehow, when she hadn't been paying attention, she'd lost most of the baby fat she'd accumulated during her pregnancy. Still, her hips were fuller. Her belly was no longer concave, but softly rounded. And her breasts...they weren't the simple, unobtrusive A-cup they'd always been, but two full sizes larger. Just looking at them made her wonder.

What did Dax think of her body now?

Even as she thought it, she blushed. She knew he saw *something* he liked, because whenever she looked at him unexpectedly, she caught him watching her with a wild, hot intensity that made her hot right back. She tried to pretend she didn't notice, but in the deep of the night she often thought about what they did to each other.

She'd been rude to him last night, inexcusably rude. He had no idea why, couldn't possibly understand how she was letting her past guide her. For most of her childhood, she'd blindly obeyed her father. She'd followed orders, squelched her need for a feminine role model and had done whatever it took to please the man.

Opinions hadn't been encouraged.

As a result, she was naturally inhibited. Being quiet and unobtrusive had been necessary for survival, as had keeping thoughts and emotions to herself. They were habits she'd carried into adulthood.

Now she was fiercely independent, and she liked it that way. Few, if any, had penetrated her protective shell.

Dax had, though, and it was scary stuff.

She dressed, then took Taylor next door to her baby-sitter, Mrs. Chapman. The woman was sixty-five and spry as a woman half her age, even if she spent her days wearing formal velvet dresses and watching soap operas. She loved Taylor with all her heart, which was enough for Amber.

On the drive to Dax's office, Amber practiced her breathing techniques and concentrated hard on calm images, but all she could think about was that one day they'd spent together, so long ago.

He would have done anything to protect her that day, and so far she'd paid him back by hiding his daughter from him and being as rude and hard to be with as possible. Something had to give, and she wasn't sure it could be her. But she had to try.

She was climbing the steps of the station, her apology on her lips, picturing a miserable and hungry Dax, when he came out.

He had a woman on each arm, and he was smiling—*grinning* actually—looking happy, confident, strikingly handsome and not even remotely miserable.

The bastard. The least he could have done was to look hungry.

The women were smiling, too, also looking happy, confident and strikingly handsome.

Any urge to apologize vaporized.

Wishing she could disappear into a great big black hole, Amber faltered, but of course it was too late to run. She was out in the open, only a few steps below them. Any second, he was going to notice her.

If he ever took his eyes off the other women, that is.

"Oh Dax," simpered the tall, thin, gorgeous blonde on his left. "This has been a long time coming."

"I know. You've been so patient." Dax smiled into her eyes. "Work's been a bear."

"All I want to know is, are you going to make the wait worthwhile?" The redhead on his right lifted a suggestive brow, making promises with her eyes that made Amber roll hers.

"Absolutely," Dax told her, still smiling.

"Good. Because..." The blonde leaned close and whispered something in his ear.

His eyebrows shot straight up.

"No secrets," pouted the redhead, pressing her lush curves against Dax.

He smiled at her, too, his eyes heavy and slumberous.

Amber gritted her teeth. They were almost on top of her now, and he was so busy with bimbette-one and bimbette-two that he hadn't even seen her!

This was the man she pictured as miserable all night because of her rudeness? *Ha!*

Since she couldn't disappear into thin air, she would have to handle this as she would any uncomfortable situation, with her famed, icy control. "Good morning, Dax," she said, ever so proud of her cool voice. She only hoped he couldn't see the steam coming out of her ears.

"Amber." He stopped short, clearly surprised. "Hello."

Amber didn't want to think about how his smile suddenly warmed, or how this time it reached his eyes. No, she didn't want to think about that, or she'd lose her anger. Anger was good here, anger would get her through. "You look awfully busy this morning."

He dropped his hold on his playmates and looked

suddenly panicked. *"Taylor.* There's nothing wrong with her..."

Well darn if that fierce worry in his expression didn't defuse a good part of her temper. "No, Taylor is fine." But since she wouldn't apologize now, she needed another reason for her appearance. Frantically she searched her mind and came up with...nothing. "I was just out for a walk and thought I'd say hello. So...hello." Forcing a smile, she turned away.

"Wait."

She didn't, couldn't.

"Amber?"

She couldn't get away fast enough, and behind her, she heard him swear.

"Amber, wait—"

Then he was there, alone, taking her arm and turning her back to face him. "Just out for a walk?" He shook his head. "Come on, Amber. What's this really about?"

For some idiotic reason, her throat closed. "I told you. I'm just walking."

He shot a doubtful look at her heels. "In those?"

Cool. Calm. That was the ticket. "Are my shoes a problem for you?"

"Not for me." He smiled angelically. "That's a pretty suit."

"Thank you."

"Personally, that short skirt could quickly become

The Harlequin Reader Service® — Here's how it works:

Accepting your 2 free books and gift places you under no obligation to buy anything. You may keep the books and gift and return the shipping statement marked "cancel." If you do not cancel, about a month later we'll send you 4 additional novels and bill you just $3.34 each in the U.S., or $3.80 each in Canada, plus 25¢ shipping & handling per book and applicable taxes if any.* That's the complete price and — compared to cover prices of $3.99 each in the U.S. and $4.50 each in Canada — it's quite a bargain! You may cancel at any time, but if you choose to continue, every month we'll send you 4 more books, which you may either purchase at the discount price or return to us and cancel your subscription.

*Terms and prices subject to change without notice. Sales tax applicable in N.Y. Canadian residents will be charged applicable provincial taxes and GST.

a favorite of mine, but it seems a waste to exercise in it."

Dignity, she reminded herself. *Keep it.* "I always walk before work. It's terrific exercise."

His look was long and knowing. "This place is at least twelve miles from your place."

"I'm in excellent shape." She glanced at the women still waiting for Dax. They had rich curves and fabulous bodies, and she found her temper again. "For a woman who's just had a baby, anyway."

"That you most definitely are." He ran a finger over her perfectly-in-place hair. "You sure look great for someone who's walked so far. Oh, and look at that..." He gestured to her car, parked on the street only fifteen feet away. "How in the world did *that* get here? Don't tell me it's trained to follow you on your morning constitutional."

"Very funny."

He grinned. She should have known better. For whatever reason, there was no controlling herself around him. "Glad I'm such a source of amusement for you. I have to go now."

"Like you did last night?"

Last night. The reason she'd come. "I'll talk to you later." No way was she going to apologize in front of an audience. "When you're not so...busy."

It was as if he could see right through her. "I'm not too busy for you." He reached for her hand. His voice was low so that only she could hear it. Only problem, the exciting, rough timbre of it sent tingles down her spine. "What's the matter, Amber? Can't you tell me?"

It was hard, she discovered, to feel his hands on her. She liked the warmth in them too much. Liked how important she felt. How special.

That she could actually let herself depend on that warmth and strength scared her.

He scared her.

Then she remembered the women. "You visiting with your sisters?" she asked casually, not wanting to publicly misjudge him again, as she had in the medical center.

Was that a flash of guilt that crossed his face as he glanced at them over his shoulder? "Ah...no. Not today."

Okay, then. "Gotta go."

"Wait—"

But she couldn't, she just couldn't.

DAX WATCHED Amber escape. His obligation, in the form of four fine legs behind him, burned. Not that Amber would have believed him if he'd told her.

Hell, half of the people he knew wouldn't believe him.

He glanced over his shoulder at the two women. In response, they both waved and giggled. Skin shimmered. Breasts jiggled.

Dax groaned, but the decision was actually easy.

He raced after Amber, catching her just as she unlocked her car.

"Amber."

She glared at him.

"Come on, baby—"

She went rigid. "I am most definitely not your *baby*. Check with the two women waiting for you. I'm sure either of them would swoon at the opportunity to be called by such an endearing term."

He had no idea why he found her stiff unyielding attitude so wildly appealing, or why he suddenly felt like grinning. "Just listen to me, that's all I'm asking."

"I'm in a hurry."

Oh yeah, she was in a hurry. But *she'd* come to *him*. And he wanted to know why. "Please?" He risked touching her again, running his fingers up and down her arm. He couldn't seem to help himself, he had to have that connection.

She went completely still. Nothing gave her away, but he just *knew* she responded to his touch. He looked into her inscrutable face and wished she'd show him how she really felt, wished he didn't have to guess. "About the women..."

"Uh-huh."

"I know what you're probably thinking."

"I doubt it." She sighed. "Dax, really. You don't have to explain why you're going on a date, much less why you're doing it in the morning, with *two* women. It's none of my business."

"It's not a date."

The two women, apparently tired of waiting, came down the stairs. The redhead smiled at Amber. "We won him in an auction." She smiled wickedly. "He's ours for the rest of the day."

"It's true." The blonde smiled, almost licking her lips in anticipation. "We can do whatever we want with him, we were promised."

Together, they grinned.

Unbelievably, Dax felt himself blush. "The auction was a long time ago," he said quickly. "And I've been too busy to meet my obligation—" This wasn't going well, he could tell by the ice in Amber's gaze. "It was to raise money for the fire stations on the west side," he added. "All the guys did it."

"But you brought in the most money," the redhead added helpfully.

"Did he now?" Amber asked coolly.

"Uh... Ladies, I'll be with you in just a moment, okay?"

Thank God they took the hint and backed off, giving him and Amber some desperately needed privacy. Only problem, he didn't have a clue as to what to say.

Amber slid on a pair of mirrored sunglasses and got into her car. "Sounds like you're in for quite a day, Dax. I'd say be good, but I already know you will be."

SOMEHOW DAX managed to escape Ginger and Cici's clutches relatively unscathed. It was mid-day by the time he did it, though. Ignoring his stacked messages and overworked secretary, he drove straight to Amber's office.

He couldn't explain his urgency or why, for the first time in the ten years he'd been participating in the bachelor auction fund-raiser, he resented the time he'd spent. All day he'd yearned to be somewhere else.

He'd wanted to be with Taylor. And okay, maybe with Amber, too, but that made no sense. Still, he couldn't get to her office fast enough, couldn't wait to try to soothe her ruffled feathers. And her feathers had most definitely been ruffled, whether she admitted it or not.

Suddenly that thought made him grin, and he loped up the stairs to the building where she worked.

Amber's secretary explained she was in a meeting and couldn't be disturbed. Dax gave her his most charming smile, but she didn't budge. Around him, the office buzzed with new listings, new sales and the general excitement of a place on the move.

Dax waited until the secretary picked up a phone before he simply strode past her desk toward Amber's closed door.

"Hey," the woman called out, "you can't just—"

Dax let himself into Amber's office and carefully shut the door on her secretary's protests.

Amber was behind her desk, a pair of reading

glasses perched on her nose, a pencil in her mouth, a phone to her ear. Her eyes were even, her hands steady, her every hair in place. She'd shed the power jacket, but the white blouse she wore was wrinkle-free, prim and proper.

Somewhere beneath that icy control lay the passion he remembered so well. He'd caught a tiny glimpse of it that morning, behind her cool facade. She'd been mad as hell at him, and mad as hell at herself for feeling that emotion in the first place.

Dax grinned again.

At the sight of him, her carefully painted mouth tightened, but that was the only outward sign he received. She didn't rush, and when she was done with her phone call, she slowly set down her pencil, removed her glasses and looked at him. "Back so soon?" Her voice was smooth and very polite. "I would have thought Barbie and Sunshine would keep you tied up for hours."

"Ginger and Cici," he corrected. "And though they were very...persuasive, I managed to escape."

"Hmmm." She bent to her work, but her knuckles went white on the pencil she gripped. "I bet."

"And how was your day?" he inquired conversationally, sitting uninvited on a chair in front of her desk.

"Busy." She glanced at him pointedly. "Still is."

Ah, the cold shoulder. "You probably didn't miss me one little bit, did you?"

"Not one little bit," she agreed.

He couldn't help it, he laughed.

Her eyes chilled several degrees. "If you don't mind..."

"Amber." He controlled himself, but the smile remained. "Admit it, you're jealous as hell."

Aghast, she stared at him. "You've been drinking."

"I don't drink."

"Then you're delusional." She leaned forward. "Just so you know, I never get jealous. Certainly not over a nitwit who enjoys dating brainless—"

"Careful," he said, laughing again. "You might prove my point."

She was still for a long beat. Then regally she rose and pointed an elegant finger at the door. "I think you should leave."

"So you can recapture that famous control?" He rose, too, and came around her desk. "I don't think so. Watching your temper rise is fascinating, Amber. In fact, *everything* about you is fascinating."

She shook her head, her composure slipping enough to show her genuine confusion. "I don't know what you want from me."

"Lots. But I'll start with this." He hauled her into his arms and kissed her. It was a stupid move, uncalculated as it was genuine, but he didn't stop.

She went still as stone, but didn't push him away. Taking that for permission, he dove into her sweet mouth, mating his tongue to hers, giving, urging, pouring everything he had into that kiss until he felt her hands open on his shoulders, then grab fistfuls of his shirt.

"Yeah, now *that's* what I've wanted all damn day," he whispered. "That and this..." He kissed her again, his hands gripping her hips, pulling her closer, then closer still.

With a little murmur of acquiescence that made him even hotter, she wrapped her arms around his neck and kissed him back until he couldn't remember his name, much less his point.

When the kiss ended, he murmured in her ear.

"The women meant nothing to me," he said. "It was an obligation, one I made months ago." Lifting his head, he looked into her eyes. "They paid big bucks. Money that will be well spent." He kissed her again. The helpless sounds of arousal she made were the most erotic he'd ever heard. "Be jealous, Amber. Wish you could take their place if you want. Kiss me stupid again if it helps. But please, don't be mad at me anymore."

She touched her wet mouth, looking shell-shocked, as if she couldn't believe how she'd lost herself. "I'm not angry," she whispered and sank into her chair. "I need to work now."

She needed to think, he realized, and he would let her because that was how she worked, and he didn't intend to rush her.

Hell, he didn't want to rush himself.

Leaning in close, he gave her one last kiss, pleased to feel her cling to him for just a second.

He was half out of her office when she called him. Turning, he looked at her over his shoulder.

"I wasn't jealous," she told him. "Much." Her mouth curved as she offered him a smile, and Dax felt the weight of the world lift off his shoulders.

8

THAT NIGHT, arms full of her briefcase, a diaper bag, dinner and Taylor, Amber let herself into her condo. Her feet were killing her and so was the whirlwind her life had become.

Going back to work had been good for her self-esteem because she was still good at it. She needed the money, too, having depleted her savings over the past year in Mexico. But balancing her wild hours with her newfound motherhood was much tougher than she could have imagined.

Naturally, before she could set a thing down, the phone rang. Dropping her purse and dinner to the counter, she freed up a hand to grab it.

"Let's start all over."

The low, sexy voice liquefied her bones. "Excuse me?"

"I want to start over," Dax said.

Amber settled the phone between her jaw and shoulder, and kicked off her heels. "From where?"

"From the beginning, but I'd settle for the night I brought you dinner. Was it good by the way?"

Amber placed Taylor in her swing. Her jacket hit a chair and relieved of all her weight, she sagged against the counter. "I suppose I should apologize for that. But yes, it was good." She paused. "So was yours."

Dax laughed softly and the sound vibrated through her body, pooling in certain erogenous spots she rarely thought about.

"I like a woman with a healthy appetite."

She thought about the smile she could hear in his voice and wondered if all the women he rescued fell for him. Probably, she admitted.

But she was above such things.

"How was lunch with my father?" she asked, purposely hardening herself. "I never got to ask you."

"Your father is a single-minded, opinionated, walking, talking ego."

"Tell me something I don't know."

"Okay... You care what he thinks of you."

How was it that he went directly to the heart of the matter every time? And how was it that she let him?

"He's also stubborn as hell," he said. "Just like his daughter."

Amber laughed, then shook her head at herself. Distance, she reminded herself. She needed to keep her distance.

Never an easy thing with this man.

She set a sleepy Taylor in motion by gently pushing the swing. "Is this why you called, to list my failings?"

"I grew up with five sisters, I know better than to list a woman's failings. But I could give you a full list of your positive attributes if you'd like. I have a most excellent memory."

Her breath caught. Laughter faded, replaced by a needy emptiness she didn't want to face. "It was a long time ago. It's best forgotten."

"I'll never forget."

Her hand stilled on Taylor's swing. "You think about sex far too much."

"Well I'm red-blooded, aren't I?"

"Yeah." He most definitely was.

"But I've told you, it was far more than just sex. Let me prove it to you."

His voice alone could convince her. She could only be thankful he wasn't here in person to add his smile, his eyes, his incredible hands to the magic.

With a sigh, she set a kettle of water on the stove. She needed tea, her own personal comfort drink. "What did you want, Dax?"

"To talk."

About their kiss? About the fact she'd nearly let it go much further than a kiss? "About?" she asked cautiously.

"Lots of stuff."

Could he really have called just to talk? With her?

"But let's start with your father."

Her stomach clenched. Of course not.

"He'd like to see Taylor sometime. I told him that was entirely up to you."

"I've offered to take her to him before," she said coolly.

"He wasn't ready. He is now."

"I suspect you had a great deal to do with that."

"I thought you'd be happy."

She *should* be, should also be grateful, but instead she only resented the fact that Dax had accomplished overnight what she hadn't been able to do it in a year's time. "I'll think about it," she said, knowing she sounded prim, polite. Difficult.

"Fair enough," he said, accepting her answer so quickly she felt suspicious.

With good reason.

"I have another favor. This one's a toughie."

She'd nearly forgotten to be leery of him! How had he done this to her, gotten her to actually almost *trust* him? "I don't care to be pushed into a decision about seeing my father."

"My favor has nothing to do with your father. I wanted you and Taylor to come with me to a barbecue tomorrow night. At my parents."

She blinked and drew a careful breath as her brain struggled to shift gears. "Why?"

"I don't know, maybe because you're the mother of my child?" He laughed at her silence. "It's not a death sentence. You go, you eat, you smile, you laugh— Wait...it doesn't hurt you to laugh, does it?"

"Sometimes." But she did it anyway as she sat at her table. "I'm sorry. I thought...well, never mind."

"You thought I was going to railroad you into doing something you don't want to do."

Yes.

"For the record," he said, his voice solemn now. "I would never, *never*, do that."

"Never is a long time, Dax."

"Yes."

"What will happen if we disagree about something?"

"What do you mean?"

She bounced up again, stalked the length of her kitchen. "You'll expect me to do things your way."

"Haven't you ever heard of give-and-take?"

"You expect me to believe you'll let me do things my way?"

"Yes! Look, I know I don't hold back much. I have a wide range of emotions, and I'm afraid I have a temper, too." His voice gentled, became disturbingly intimate. "But I'd never hurt you, Amber. It's not a stretch for me to make that promise. It shouldn't be a stretch for *anyone* to make you that promise."

"Yeah well, you'd be surprised."

"I wish we were having this conversation in person. So that I could touch you while I tell you all this."

Heat, the kind he always seemed to cause within her, warmed her from head to toe. "That's... probably not wise."

"When I touch you, you let down that guard. When I kiss you, you let go even more. You let me see the *real* you."

She took a deep breath because suddenly she

couldn't seem to get enough air, but the yearning deep inside her didn't fade.

"I like that real you, Amber."

She let out a disparaging sound and sat down again. "I never know what to say to you."

"Say you believe me. That you believe in us."

"There is no us."

As if he heard her panic, he softened his voice even more. "Us as in Taylor's parents."

"That's all."

"That's the most important," he agreed. "For now. You and Taylor, you can depend on me, Amber. That's a promise, and I've never broken one yet."

No one had ever made her a promise and kept it.

"What do you think, Amber? Can I pick you and Taylor up tomorrow night. At six? You'll have a great time."

"Another promise."

"Absolutely."

She swallowed hard, fighting her vulnerability with every ounce of strength she possessed. It helped to glance over and see Taylor sleeping peacefully. Happy and content. "Tomorrow, then," she whispered, and hung up before Dax could question the quiver in her voice.

Drawing in a deep, cleansing breath, Amber beat back her emotions. It was a lifelong habit.

Then she fought her fears the best way she knew how, with food. Lots of it.

THE NEXT NIGHT, at nearly six o'clock, Amber stood in a bra and panties contemplating her closet. She'd been looking at her wardrobe for an embarrassing hour now. "A barbecue," she muttered.

What did one wear to such an event?

Jeans, she decided, with a shrug that would have told anyone watching that she couldn't care less.

But she *did* care, too much. She wanted to look good for a man she hadn't wholly decided to let herself care for.

She slipped into the jeans and stared at herself. They were too tight, thanks to her just-given-birth-three-months-ago body, but she didn't own a larger size.

Fine, so she wouldn't wear jeans. With another shrug, she yanked them off. But her khakis had some sort of stain on them, one that could be directly related to Taylor. Her wool trousers were far too dressy.

Dressy, she could have handled. But this was a family party. Silk and stockings weren't required.

And wasn't that just the problem?

She tossed her wool trousers over her shoulder to join her other discarded clothing on the floor and stood in front of the mirror. "It's not the clothes," she admitted out loud. It was the evening ahead that had her nerves in a riot.

There.

She'd admitted it.

Her bout of anxiety had nothing to do with *where* she was going, it was *who* she was going with.

Dax did this to her, damn him, caused this butterfly dance low in her belly. "And the mess in this room is his fault, too," she decided, looking around at the cyclone she'd wrought. Nearly everything she owned was in a pile on the floor.

The doorbell rang.

She froze. "Oh my God." Galvanized into action, she threw on a denim skirt and shoved her arms into a white button-up, long-sleeved shirt. Last minute panic time was over. She'd have to make do as she was.

Her usually perfectly groomed hair was wild. So were her dark eyes. She had no idea where the flush on her cheeks came from, but it made her look...young. *Too* young.

And the shirt, good Lord. White had not been the wisest choice, only emphasizing her new bra size.

The doorbell rang again and she dashed out of her room, past the second bedroom where Taylor lay sleeping and down the hall.

Her heart was pounding.

No rush, she told herself, and purposely stopped to draw in a deep, calming breath. She was fine.

Just fine.

When she believed it, when she had some semblance of calm, she opened the door.

And immediately lost it again.

Dax was leaning against the jamb, looking shockingly desirable. He wore jeans and a long-sleeved shirt the exact color of his baby blue eyes.

Those eyes smiled into hers as he leaned close, and any semblance of calm flew right out the window. His scent assaulted her; clean, woodsy, and all male. Then her breath backed up in her throat because he was so close she almost—*almost*—tipped toward him.

She wanted a kiss.

Startled, she just looked at him, specifically at that mouth that she knew could drive her crazy. No. No kiss, she decided hastily. She couldn't handle it, not now, not when her control was already long gone.

"Hey," he said, moving even closer, and her heart stumbled. His sleepy, heavy-lidded eyes met hers for one long, silent moment.

Please, was her only, suddenly shocking thought. *Kiss me.*

As if he could hear her, his long lashes lowered over his eyes, his mouth brushed her jaw.

Yes, *yes*, he was going to do it, thank God, for she wanted that with every fiber of her being. Forget control, forget distance, she wanted his kiss. *Now.*

Softly, gently, his lips slid over her cheek, nipped at her throat and then...he straightened away from her. "You're here. I thought maybe you'd changed your mind."

"No." She had to clear her throat. "I'm ready. I...just need to get Taylor."

His grin was more than a little wicked. "You're happy to see me."

She managed a laugh. "Not really."

"Another lie." He tsked. "Santa's going to take you off his list." Then he smiled slow and sure. "You wanted me to kiss you."

"In your dreams."

His laugh was just as wicked as his grin. "Oh, you're most definitely in my dreams."

His eyes were so hot, so sure and knowing, she swallowed hard. "I'll get Taylor."

His gaze dipped down to her mouth, then further still, slowly running over her body in a way that might have, if she'd been a weaker woman, left her legs wobbly.

She locked her knees just in case.

"I've never seen you in anything other than a power suit," he said huskily. "I like the change."

She resisted, barely, the urge to tug at her snug shirt.

He reached for her hand. "You know, I'm beginning to think I'm getting the hang of reading your eyes. They're so expressive they give you away, especially right now."

Could he see then, how uncomfortable she was? How self-conscious?

"You look beautiful, Amber," he said, his gaze directly on hers.

Yes, apparently he could.

"I mean it," he said silkily, and for once, she believed him.

THE MCCALL house was packed with smiling, laughing, talking people, not to mention barking dogs and a blaring stereo. Halfway up the walk, Amber faltered. If this had been a business gathering, she would have known exactly what to do and how to act.

But this wasn't a work function. This wasn't a required cocktail party or fund-raiser. It was supposed to be fun.

She didn't do fun very well.

She'd counted on using Taylor as a shield, but Dax had the baby secure in his arms, and she looked so content Amber had little choice but to leave her there.

Through the opened gate to the backyard the party looked to be in full swing. Couples danced, kids played, people talked. Everywhere.

Amber just stared at what seemed like a sea of hundreds, all happy and comfortable and having a good time. "Are *all* these people your family?"

"And friends."

"It's..." *Loud*, came to mind, but that seemed rude. Yet she was incapable of coming up with a proper white lie since her stomach was suddenly in her throat. "Different."

"I should tell you now, my family is bossy, nosy and opinionated."

Gee, there was a surprise. "I'm sure I can handle it." But she wasn't sure at all. She had no experience with large families, no experience with families period.

Dax looked at the hand she'd unconsciously placed on her jittery stomach, and placed his own over hers. "They're going to love you, Amber. They're just going to be loud and nosy about it."

The very idea of perfect strangers falling in love with her was as ridiculous as...well, as being at this party.

"They will." He smiled, that special one he seemed to hold in reserve just for her. "Ready?"

"Yes. No. Yes. God. I don't know." It *was* the twenty-first century, but having a child out of wedlock didn't feel like something to be particularly proud of, no matter what the circumstances.

Would they resent her?

Think that she'd trapped Dax on purpose?

Why had she agreed to this?

"I have no idea what's running through that head of yours," Dax said with a low laugh. "But I promise it isn't going to be half as bad as whatever you're thinking."

"Okay." She straightened her shoulders resolutely. "Let's do it."

Laughing again, Dax shook his head. "It's not a firing squad, either. It's going to be fun." A sigh escaped him when none of the tension left her. "Come on, I can see you're not going to relax until we get it over with."

With Taylor snug and happy in one arm, and his other hand firmly holding hers, he drew them into the fray.

They were immediately surrounded.

"Dax! Let me have that baby!" The woman Amber recognized as Suzette pushed her way to the front and took Taylor into her arms. "Oh, she's beautiful!" She turned a smile on Amber. "Nice to see you again, we're so glad you could come. Dax has told us all about you."

Amber shot a look at Dax, wondering what exactly he'd told them about her.

He just lifted a brow and smiled, leaving her clueless, which she was quite certain he knew she hated.

"Taylor is such a good baby." Suzette sighed dreamily. "I can't wait to see mine." She patted her huge belly. "If he or she ever decides to come on out! I'm two weeks overdue now." She kissed Taylor's little nose.

Another woman pressed close, looking so much like Suzette that Amber blinked.

"Hey there, Dax." The woman kissed him, then leaned over Suzette and kissed Taylor, too. "Hey, sweetie."

Taylor drooled her pleasure and let out her characteristic squeal, which meant, "I like this! Gimme more!"

Everyone laughed.

"Give her to me, Suzette," the new woman said. "She likes me best anyway."

"This is Shelley," Dax informed Amber. "My oldest and most bossy sister."

"Honestly, Dax, you know perfectly well *I'm* the bossy one." Another blond, beautiful woman pushed her way through the crowd.

"Amy." Dax grinned and endured her bear hug and loud smacking kiss right on the mouth. "And you're right, it's a tie. Amber, this is Amy. The baby of the clan."

"I'm not the baby, you are!" But she smiled widely at Taylor, snatched Taylor from Shelley's arms and reached out an arm to give Amber a brief hug. "Wonderful to meet you, welcome to the family."

Hopelessly awkward and yet unbearably touched at the same time, Amber's heart tied itself into knots. The strange tightness in her chest, the one she associated with Dax, was back. Actually, it hadn't left since she'd first seen him again.

Hormones, she told herself. That's all it was.

"Let me in, let me in!" The woman that pushed her way though this time had definitely been blond before the gray had taken over. She came only to Dax's chest, was twice as wide, and had a face filled with joy and excitement.

She went straight for Taylor. "Let me have that precious little bundle of love! Hand her over to grandma right this instant!"

"That 'precious little bundle' smells to high

heaven," Dax warned as Taylor was passed yet again. "She needs to be changed."

"What, like I've never changed a diaper? Yours included."

"Just giving you fair warning, Mom."

"Hey there, precious," she cooed to Taylor, who all but soaked up the attention.

Then Dax's mother turned with an expectant smile to Amber.

"Amber, this is my mother," Dax said. "Emily McCall. And watch out, she's—"

"Happy to meet you," Emily interrupted smoothly. "My goodness, you're lovely! I hope you like meat, you're so thin for just having had a baby! Are you eating enough? *Thomas!*" she yelled, without waiting for an answer. She gestured wildly to the tall, darkly handsome man working the barbecue. "Thomas, get over here and meet the mother of your newest granddaughter. And bring a fully loaded plate!"

"Oh no, I couldn't—" Amber protested, only to be hushed by Emily.

Thomas arrived, carting food and a pleasant smile. "Hello."

Amber held out her hand. Thomas took it, and then gently drew her in for a warm hug. "Welcome," he said, in the same silky rough voice as his son.

He'd hugged her, was all Amber could think. As if she belonged to the family. The casual, easy, genuine affection startled her. She wanted to somehow savor it, and at the same time, wanted to run for the hills. Hard and fast. "Uh...I've got to—"

"Eat," Emily said smoothly, ignoring the panic that surely they all could see. "She's got to eat. And drink, too." She openly eyed Amber's breasts. "You *are* breast-feeding that baby I hope."

Heat raced over Amber's cheeks, but before she could reply, Dax broke in. "Mom. You promised."

"So I meddle," she said, tossing her hands up. "I can't help it, it's my job." Then she smiled so warmly, so openly that Amber never saw it coming. "You need some meat on those bones, girl. Never mind Thomas and Dax, I can't trust them to feed you right. Come with me."

At this, both Thomas and Dax grinned, and Amber couldn't help but imagine her own father, and what his reaction to this little, bossy, demanding, nosy, wonderful woman would be.

One thing she'd always secretly admired about her father was his strength. But at that moment, he would have looked at both Dax and Thomas, at the way they allowed Emily to run their lives, and he'd have instantly labeled them as weak, spineless and insignificant.

And yet nothing could have been further from the truth.

Dax and Thomas were confident, strong-willed men. And she knew exactly how stubborn Dax could be. She suspected his father was the same.

Neither man was weak, not by any means. She

was beginning to think maybe it took more fortitude than weakness to allow all members of a family to be equal.

Emily smiled innocently as she continued to railroad Amber with all the subtly of a bull in a china shop. "Are you drinking a full glass of water every hour?"

"Oh. Well, I—"

"Maybe you're working too hard. Are you managing to get enough sleep? A baby can be so hard on a mother."

"I told you she was nosy and bossy," Dax said over his mother's head.

"Hush you! I told you to scat." Emily kissed Taylor and passed her back to Dax. "So scat!" Then she took Amber's hand. "You come with me now, honey."

Short of being rude, Amber couldn't resist. She shot a helpless glance over her shoulder at Dax, who just grinned.

No help there.

Then he was swallowed up by the crowd and Amber was left with the petite powerhouse that was Dax's mother.

9

AMBER WAS QUIET on the drive home, thinking about the glimpse she'd had into Dax's world.

She'd seen him playful and teasing with his nieces and nephews. Tolerant and protective of his sisters. Loving and warm with his parents.

Then, without warning, he'd cornered her in the foyer against a wall and had kissed her senseless. By the time he'd lifted his head, smiled wickedly and backed away, she'd nearly melted to the floor.

Who was this man, the one who could go from sweet and nurturing, to shatteringly erotic in a nanosecond? It was a sharp reminder of how different they were, for Amber couldn't imagine letting her emotions run her the way Dax did.

Inside her condo, Amber put a sleeping Taylor in her crib, then occupied herself starting a fire in the living room fireplace.

Dax waited until she had the flames flickering before he tugged her up, turning her around to face him. In an easy show of affection, he tucked a strand of hair behind her ear and smiled into her eyes. "Hey."

She tried to move back from him because being in

such proximity always made thinking difficult, but he held her in a gentle grip of steel. "Hey back," she said, trying to look as if being held by such a gorgeous man was an everyday occurrence.

"Talk to me, Amber."

"About?"

"You."

The way he looked at her, the way he spoke...as if she were the most important person in his life.... It took her breath away.

"You and your family," she said inanely. "You're very close."

"Yes. Very." He cocked his head and studied her. "Is that what's bothering you? That my family gets along?"

"You laugh, you fight, you..."

"*Love.* Is that it?"

He understood, she could hear it in his voice. Fearing his pity, she couldn't quite meet his gaze.

"I know your father isn't quite the same as mine," he said carefully.

"Nor was my mother the same as yours."

"You've not said much about her," he murmured, still close, still touching. Always touching.

"There's not much to say. She left when I was born." With long-practiced skill, she shrugged. It no longer mattered. It shouldn't matter.

"She missed raising a pretty wonderful daughter."

"I did fine without her."

His eyes were soft and unusually dark. "Yeah. You did. But you shouldn't have had to. You should have had her to talk to, to hold you. To love you."

"Love wasn't a huge priority in my household."

"Another shame, but it's not yours." He lifted her face and studied her until she squirmed. "Are you listening, Amber? *Really* listening? I get the idea you somehow think it's your fault your parents are jerks."

"No, not jerks. My father never beat me, or forgot to feed me, or anything like that. He took care of me."

"So he gave you the basics. Big deal. Parenthood is a lot harder than that, and you know it. He failed you. Your mother failed you. Your fiancé failed you, and in a way, I've failed you by not being there when you needed me, when you were having Taylor."

"That was hardly your fault," she reminded him.

"Still, I won't fail you again."

He was deadly serious and more than a little intimidating. "I don't want to be a responsibility to you," she said slowly. "I won't have you come to resent me."

"Trust me," he murmured. "It's much more than that." His thumb brushed over her lower lip and when she shivered, his eyes darkened even more. "So you were alone for most of your life with a man who obviously hadn't a clue how to show his emotions. Do you have any idea how amazing your passion is, in spite of all that?"

She laughed, then stopped short when he didn't smile, just looked at her steadily. "I don't think of myself as particularly...passionate."

"No?" His gaze dropped, ran slowly over every inch of her, leaving a rising heat everywhere it touched. "You should."

"I'd like to think I'm not run by such an emotion."

"Ah, and I am." His lips quirked. "Is that it?"

Dammit, she was amusing him. She pushed at his hand, which was still on her face, but he merely tipped up her chin, his long, warm fingers scorching her skin. "Your father told me what he thought of your mother. How he was always afraid you'd be like her."

"I see. The two of you sat around and discussed me."

"You came up a few times."

When she took a step back, he followed, his big hands tender and gentle as he reached for her. "I'm on to you, you know."

She slapped his hands away and stepped back again. "I haven't a clue what you're talking about."

"You're not like her, Amber, you never could be."

Determined to avoid this, she took one more step and hit the wall. "No I'm not, because I'm so careful." *Usually.* "I've always been, but somehow, with you..." His hands caged her in, her breath backed up in her throat. "Somehow you make me forget to watch myself."

"Really? That's interesting." One of his hands slid

down her side now, and since her shirt came to the waistband of her skirt and wasn't tucked in, his fingers slipped under and touched bare skin. "Always so in control." His thumb slid over her belly and she drew in a shaky breath. "And yet not with me. Could you have feelings for me then? Deep ones?" That hand danced around now to her back, and his thumb made a lazy circle very low on her spine, causing a shiver.

The flare of desire in his eyes didn't help. "Dax—"

Those magical fingers played lightly over her tingling flesh. She held her breath when he splayed his big, warm hand over her bottom, pressing her to him so that she could feel his erection.

"You don't want to feel anything for me," he said huskily. "But I feel something for you. Can you feel what I'm feeling, Amber?"

Oh yeah. He was huge, pulsing against her.

"Can you?"

"I...yes." Definitely yes.

"Today scared you."

She stared at him, and he stared back, achingly patient, silently demanding her honesty.

"A little, maybe. All of you. All that passion, all that wild jubilance."

"And all that unpredictability. You don't know what to make of me, do you Amber? Or what to expect?"

"No."

"You hate that."

"Yes." But she looked at his mouth and a part of her burned for it to touch hers, fear be damned, all the while aware of how turned on he was. How turned on *she* was.

"What's between us is a work in progress," he said. "It can go as you want. You can be in control." He nudged even closer. "Or not."

"Is there really an 'us'?"

"Yeah," Dax whispered huskily, no longer surprised by that very fact. "There's an *us*." To show her, he took her mouth with his, the promise echoing in his head as he tasted her.

She kissed him back, but then put a shaking hand to his chest. "I'm not ready for this. For you."

Neither was he, no matter what a certain body part was screaming. "No rush."

"Okay. Good." She licked her already wet lips in a self-conscious gesture he was certain she didn't mean to make so damn sexy.

"We could just let this attraction sit in the driver's seat," he said. "And see where it takes us."

"I feel as though I should pull over and ask for directions."

He smiled. "Do we need a map then?"

"I do, yes. I need a plan."

"You can't always plan matters of the heart, I'm learning." He set his forehead to hers. "You're my case in point."

Her dark eyes were liquid and full of unmistakable yearning. He wished, just once, that she would speak of that yearning, instead of fighting it.

Then she closed her eyes.

"No fair hiding." He touched his lips to the corner of her mouth, hovering there, thrilling to her quick intake of breath. "Look at me."

Both her eyes and her mouth opened slightly, and she leaned toward him, clearly wanting, expecting, needing a kiss. "Dax…"

"Tell me what you want, Amber."

Instead, she shifted closer, dropped her gaze to his lips.

"With words." He smiled wickedly. "It's your plan, you're the one in control, remember?"

"You want me to say it."

She sounded so scandalized he nearly laughed. "Yeah." Softly, in a barely there touch, he kissed the other side of her mouth.

She moaned, and the sound made him hot. "Tell me."

Pleasure sighed out of her when he slid his fingers into her hair, but though she turned into him, pressed her body to his, she remained silent.

He drew back.

She let out an exploding sigh. "Okay! Kiss me, dammit!"

"If you insist," he murmured demurely.

The connection was combustive, instantly sizzling, and there was no way to hold back his low growl of helpless arousal, no way he wanted to.

Already it wasn't enough. The kiss wasn't enough.

Threading his fingers through her silky soft hair, he angled her for a deeper, hotter, wetter kiss. Their bodies swayed together. He could feel her breasts against his chest, her belly flat to his, and when he rocked slowly, melding their hips into a perfect fit so that he could feel the heat between her thighs, he nearly died right there. "If you need a road map to my feelings here," he murmured. "Let me assure you, I want more."

Her breath wasn't any more steady when she met his gaze warily. "How much more?"

He wanted it all. He wanted her to willingly shed that cool, calm control to give him the real Amber beneath. "You know how much I want. Now tell me what *you* want."

She loosened a fist from his hair, then smoothed that hand over his chest, from one side to another, and just that light touch sent his head spinning.

"Words," he said. "Tell me in words."

"I want..." Helplessly, she lifted her head. "You. But I don't know what to do."

"Are we talking about a physical want?"

She nodded.

If it had been any other woman telling him they wanted him, it would have made Dax's evening.

But this wasn't any other woman, it was Amber, and he suddenly wanted far more than her physical want. Swallowing his disappointment, he let out a laugh. "I remember you knowing exactly what to do before."

Her body was taut and quivering as he kissed her this time, telling him plainly what her mouth seemed to be struggling with, and heat roared through his veins. He caressed her slim back, up and down, slowly, fingers spread wide so he could touch as much of her as possible. She did the same, running her hands all over him. Then, slowly, he ended the kiss.

Her eyes were huge on his. "What?"

"I just wanted to make sure you're still in the driver's seat. I know how important that is to you."

He'd been only teasing, but she frowned, seriously considering. "I'm okay. I think." She looked at him. "More."

"Mmm. Aggressive." He stroked his hands down her hips, past her thighs, to the hem of her skirt, then skimmed them back up again, beneath the material now, to...ah, those legs. At the feel of lace, then soft, bare thighs, he groaned.

She squirmed and looked defensive. "They're more comfortable then regular nylons."

"Thank God for comfort."

"And they don't seem to snag like the others—"

"And thriftiness, too."

"They're very practical, you know."

He laughed. "You can't be thinking I don't like them."

"I— You do?"

"I do. Is it okay that they turn me on?" He had to laugh again when she considered.

"Why don't you just enjoy the reaction you're getting from me...?" He slid his hips to hers and lowered his lips to her ear. "Feel what you do to me."

She gripped him tight and nodded.

"More, Amber?"

"Yes, please," she whispered politely, making him crack up again. He'd never in his life laughed while trying to get a woman naked. He liked it. And her. Very much.

"Still so in control..." He continued to stroke her, determined to shatter her restraint. "Touch me back," he urged.

Her hands slipped beneath his shirt, streaking over his bare back. "Dax—" Her hips undulated against his. "Where's my more?"

That needy, whispery voice nearly brought him to his knees. "Here." His voice was rough. "Skin to skin this time, I want to feel you, all of you."

Apparently in agreement, she tore off his shirt, then sucked in her breath. "You didn't tell me how beautiful *you* are." Her fingertips slid over his chest, her eyes wide with awe.

"Not like you." He had his own ogling to do now as he undid the buttons on her blouse, then slid it down to her elbows. At the sight of her, he let out his own shaky breath, then bent to her. "Oh, baby, not like you." Opening his mouth against her, he scattered hot little nips over her quivering skin. "Amber...you still okay?"

"What?" Dazed, she lifted her head, her arms still trapped by her blouse.

Through the white lace of her bra, her nipples were puckered and begging for attention, which he intended to give. "I asked if you were all right. You didn't want to lose yourself, remember?" Cupping her breasts, he let his thumbs glance over the tips, back and forth as her eyes glazed over. "I don't want to take this further than you want."

"I..." She closed her eyes when he continued that movement with his thumbs, then slid her hands up around his neck, and squeezed him so he could scarcely breath. "I'm fine. Just don't stop."

He might have grinned, but he was having trouble with his breathing. The feel of her in his hands...

"Give me my more, Dax."

Laughing softly he tugged her shirt completely off. Hunger and need pumped through him. It wasn't comforting to realize that he would be only partially sated by making love with her tonight.

The fire was roaring, warm and enticing, and they sank to the thick rug in front of it. He expected some hesitation when he opened his arms, but she came right into them, fitting there as if she belonged forever.

Forever.

What a thought. He'd never believed in forever, at

least not for himself. "Still okay?" he asked, running a finger down her body.

She sucked in a breath when he slid off the rest of her clothes, then his. "Yes."

"Just wanted to make sure." He played with her belly button, her hipbone, then her inner thigh, which had her letting that air back out again, through her teeth. When he lingered there, she made that needy little whimper deep in her throat. "You're still in control, right?"

"Dax?"

"Yeah?"

"Shut up."

He grinned, then leaned over her.

The kiss was long, wet, hot and left him aching for more. Levering himself up on his forearms, he cupped her face. "I want you, Amber. Want me back."

She arched up. "Yes."

He felt the wetness between her legs which she spread to accommodate his, but he needed the words. "Tell me."

She licked her dry lips and writhed against him, encouraging him to sink inside her, still saying nothing.

"Tell me." He stroked himself against her and her eyes went opaque.

"I want you, Dax."

He had a second to wish she'd said she *needed* him, but his body was hard and pulsing, poised for entry and aroused beyond the point of no return. When she reared up and hugged him to her, his heart squeezed.

"I have a condom this time," he said hoarsely, and when he finally managed to get it on, he drove them straight to paradise.

AMBER STIRRED first. Her body was a stranger to her, languid and lazy and newly tender in spots she'd almost forgotten about.

Oh, and she was wrapped in warm, solid arms.

It was still dark. Dax lay beside her, his breathing slow and deep and even.

For one weak moment, she let herself sink into him, into the heat and warmth and joy of his big body, enjoying the feeling of being secure and cared for.

In that moment she didn't have to be strong, she didn't have to be in charge, and she reveled in the letting go.

But she didn't fool herself; it couldn't last.

In the end, she had only herself to depend on. No matter how much Dax insisted he wanted to be there for her and Taylor, she could see fear lurking deep in his gaze.

A fear that matched hers.

He'd been so right, she thought, her heart hitching. There was no road map when it came to matters of the heart, no directions to follow.

And God help her, she was hopelessly lost.

10

WHEN DAX WOKE UP the next morning, he had an armful of warm, naked woman, a raging erection and a grin on his face.

"I could get used to this," he murmured, turning, tucking Amber beneath him. They were in her bedroom, in her bed. He'd carried her there himself sometime during the middle of the most erotic night of his life.

As her eyes fluttered open, he made his move, swooping down to take her mouth before she could utter a word. A sensuous, sleepy murmur escaped her throat and she rubbed languidly against him, returning his kiss with such heat and passion he groaned.

At the sound, she went perfectly still.

Dax raised his head. "Hey there."

She blinked slowly, looking confused, her usually perfect hair wild and willful.

Because he couldn't help it, he went for that creamy skin at the base of her neck. "Do you have any idea how sexy you are?" he asked.

She lay sprawled and gorgeous, a feast for his eyes. While he nibbled at her neck, his fingers found a velvety nipple that quickly responded to his touch. "Mmmm. You taste better than breakfast."

Her eyes closed again, her head fell back. Her breath came in little pants, quickening when he switched to her other breast. He took his time there, as well, and skimmed a hand down her belly and lower. Finding her deliciously hot, and so wet he moaned, he sank a finger into her. He played in and out of that slippery heat, his eyes crossing with lust when she clamped her legs around his hand, holding him to her.

"I'm not going anywhere," he promised, kissing her lips, her jaw, her ear. He took the sensitive lobe into his mouth and bit gently as his fingers danced over her.

She arched up into his palm, whimpering every time he withdrew. "Yeah," he whispered. "Feels good, doesn't it?"

"Dax?"

"I'm right here, Amber. Always."

Her eyes flew open again. *"Dax?"*

Hadn't they already established that? "Still me." He rose up on an elbow to study her. "Amber, are you awake?"

Again that slow blink. "I had this dream that we..." She licked her lips. "I guess it wasn't a dream."

She was adorable, he decided, slowly shaking his head. And most definitely *not* a morning person. "Not a dream."

She groaned.

"Regrets?"

"I don't feel comfortable with this type of a relationship."

"You felt comfortable enough during the night," he pointed out. "Three times, in fact."

She blushed and looked away. "Five," she muttered.

"Well then..." He grinned. "Why don't we go for an even dozen?" But when he leaned close with wicked intent, she put a hand to his chest.

He sighed and sat up. She had the entire sheet—who knew what had happened to the rest of the bedding—which left him stark naked, but he didn't care. "You still have a problem with us."

She darted him a glance. "When you say 'us' like that, it makes me nervous."

"Join the club."

"You don't look nervous, you look..." She paused, and in an unusually revealing gesture of vulnerability, she bit her lower lip. "You look hungry. As if you could eat me up for breakfast."

"In one bite."

"We're very different," she said softly. "I need time to think."

"No, you need time to control your emotions. To distance yourself from me. It really scares me how easily you can do that."

"And it scares me how much of me you see, how much you understand."

"Yeah, I understand you. Maybe someday you'll understand me back."

Eyes stricken, she opened her mouth, but Taylor chose that moment to cry out.

"She's my alarm clock," Amber said with a shaky laugh. She still held the sheet to her chin, and somehow managed to get out of the bed and keep herself covered. "She'll need to be changed and fed. I'm sorry, Dax."

It was beyond him how she could look as ravaged and luscious as she did, yet so prim and proper at the same time. The heady combination threatened his sanity. "I'm sorry, too."

AMBER SAT in the little café across the street from her office, contemplating her day. It could have been a better one.

Yesterday she'd lost a deal when a client had backed out of a sale at the last moment. Harried over that and the ensuing chaos, she'd forgotten to pick up her dry-cleaning, which had left her with nothing to wear but her now slightly too small red suit.

Despite the unseasonably warm weather, she'd been forced to keep the jacket on all day, which only emphasized her new cleavage. But at least it hid the indecently tight blouse and skirt.

The client she'd seen that morning had certainly appreciated her problem. It had taken most of their meeting to assure him she *didn't* combine business and pleasure.

In hopes of improving her mood, she sat with a bowl of frozen yogurt. At least she was finally cooling off. The pleasant buzz of people around lulled her. She took a huge bite filled with delicious strawberries and leaned back with a sigh as it melted down her parched throat.

"The way you eat that looks positively sinful."

Dax bent over her, his mouth close to her ear, so that the low, sexy timbre sent shivers racing down her spine. "Did you know you've got every male customer in this place hard as a rock, just from watching you enjoy that thing?"

"Where's Taylor?" she asked, pleased her voice sounded so steady. She wasn't about to let him know he'd made her bones dissolve.

"Mom's spoiling her for us."

Mom's spoiling her for us. So intimate. As if Amber herself was also a part of his family.

Dax helped himself to the seat next to her, leaned back and made himself at home. Faded denim snugged his long, powerful legs, though she had no idea why she noticed. His T-shirt invited her to Fear Nothing. "I take it you're off-duty."

He grinned. "Yep. I'm going to take Taylor for a picnic. Want to come?"

"You're taking a baby on a picnic? She'll eat the ants and get itchy from the grass and—"

"Amber." He laughed. "I want to take *you* on a picnic. I'm shamelessly using our daughter as an excuse."

"Oh." Another huge bite of frozen yogurt helped her stall, but she stopped when she realized Dax's gaze was riveted to her mouth. His body seemed tense, his muscles tight beneath his shirt. And oh Lord, she'd have to be totally naive to miss the bulge behind the button fly of his Levi's.

"Take some mercy on me, Amber," he said with a groan. "Either stop eating that thing as though you were in the throes of an orgasm or toss it. You're killing me."

"Hmm."

"Was that an apology?"

"I refuse to apologize because you can't keep your mind out of your pants." Gathering her briefcase, purse and yogurt—she wasn't about to give that up for him!—she rose. "I'm going back to work."

"Amber. Come on, wait up—"

When she kept going, she heard him swear behind her, heard the scrape of his chair as he came to his feet.

She moved faster.

They didn't speak as she practically ran across the street and into her building, but when she entered her office and tried to shut the door behind her, she was stymied by a one-hundred-and-eighty pound block wall.

Half in, half out, with the door nearly cutting off his nose, he grinned down at her. "You're nuts about me, I can tell."

She groaned and backed away from the door. "I'm

only letting you in because I can't stand the sight of blood. That, and my secretary, Nancy, is watching." She plopped into her chair and glared at him.

He shut the door behind him, then set a lean hip on the corner of her desk. "Let me see," he said, reaching for her spoon. "If it's as good as it looks...hmmm." His tongue darted out to catch a drop. "Oh yeah. It is."

So rattled by the sight of his wet tongue sliding over his own lips, Amber lost every thought in her head. Her hands loosened with the loss of blood flow to her brain, and the small bit of frozen yogurt still left in the cup spilled out...right down the front of her jacket.

Dax was there in a flash, laughing, slipping her jacket off her shoulders.

"No, don't," she gasped, gripping the edges of her jacket, pressing it to her too-tight blouse. "I want it on—"

"Hurry," he urged, tugging the jacket from her shoulders, leaving her exposed in nothing but the blouse she didn't want anyone to see. "Before it gets on your—" Abruptly, Dax stopped talking.

Stopped breathing.

He couldn't help himself, she was incredible. Yes, he'd already seen her, seen everything. He'd touched and licked and kissed every inch of her, but that didn't stop his heart from constricting and certain other parts of his anatomy from standing at attention at the sight of her straining against the tight confines of her white silk blouse.

"I wanted that on," she grumbled, crossing her arms over her chest.

He hardly heard her, could hardly think, but he *had* to touch.

Her face remained cool, impassive as he slid his fingers over her, but at the base of her neck, her pulse drummed wildly, giving her away.

"I'm sorry," he whispered, watching her nipples harden, pressing for freedom against the fabric. "But you're so beautiful, you stun me."

"We agreed we're too different for this," Amber said, not quite steadily, tightening her arms in front of her.

All it did was emphasize her glorious body, and the breasts she seemed embarrassed of. "No, *you* agreed."

She gave him a hot look.

It was filled with such frustration, he had to smile. "Okay, we agreed that you think *you* need space in order to protect your emotions from me."

"I don't think it, I know it."

And so did he. Dammit, so did he. "I shouldn't have come." He shoved his fingers through his hair and backed away.

"I'm sorry."

"For which?" At the door, he spun around. "For driving me crazy, or for driving me crazy slowly?"

That comment had anger flashing in her eyes. "I'm sorry you're upset that you're not getting your way."

"What's my way? Do you even know?"

"You want to have a...a fling."

That stopped him cold and he stalked back toward her. "Why don't you just marry me, dammit, and settle once and for all what I really want."

11

AMBER GAWKED at him and, in truth, Dax couldn't blame her. He was shocked, too. After that first time when he'd so foolishly asked her to marry him, he'd vowed not to think about it again.

But he knew now how he felt about being a father to Taylor. He wanted to do it right. Part-time wasn't right, not in his opinion.

He also knew how he felt about Amber, knew it was permanent, not some passing phase.

He knew this, just as he knew he'd been using her resistance to fuel his own, using it to mask his own fear of commitment.

But that was cowardly. The deep emotions he had for Amber were here to stay, and he would face them.

He had to convince her to do the same.

"Did you just..." She gazed at him helplessly, her head going back in forth in an automatic denial that had his jaw so tight he could barely breathe. "Did you..."

"Yes. For the second time. And I have to tell you, that frightened, trapped-doe look is not quite the response I was hoping for."

The look disappeared instantly as she veiled her thoughts from him.

"I told you before," she said slowly. "It's unnecessary. Nothing's changed."

"That's not an answer," he said grimly. "An answer would be 'yes, I'll make your wildest fantasies come true,' or 'no, let me rip out your heart.'"

"You're being impossible."

"Yes," he snapped. "We've already established that I'm wildly emotional, temperamental and overly sensitive. That I can't control any of that. I'm also, apparently, impossible. But I want to marry you. I want to be a family. So answer the damn question."

He couldn't have handled this any worse, and he knew it. Thanks to his own stupidity, he'd backed her into a corner with no way out. But he wouldn't withdraw the question, not when he'd put his pride on the line.

In control now, Amber didn't even blink.

"It's that tough, huh?"

"It's not as though we've had the most conventional of relationships," she told him in a tone that said she expected him to be reasonable.

He wasn't in the mood for reasonable. "Of course this relationship hasn't been normal, not from the very beginning! We met under extraordinary circumstances, for God's sake, and we've been through things other people haven't." He lifted his hands helplessly. "Nothing's been the same since that earthquake, and nothing's been the same since I met you." Dropping his hands, he shook his head. "I held you when I thought we were going to die, Amber, and yes, that was a long time ago, and yes, now everything's different. I see things differently, I feel differently." He reached for her, touched her pale face. "I have never regretted what happened. You have to know, you and Taylor are the best things that ever happened to me."

She turned away and scrubbed at the yogurt stain with a napkin. Though the stain didn't come off, she slipped the jacket back on anyway. Buttoning it, her back to him, she softly said, "You scare me."

"Does it help to know you scare me, too?"

"Actually, 'scare' isn't a strong enough word," she clarified. "*Terrify* works better."

He came up behind her, torturing himself with the feel of her spine and curved bottom against his chest and groin.

At the contact, her fingers fumbled on her buttons.

Reaching around her, he brushed her hands away and took over the task. "It's not like you to be so fidgety."

"I'm nervous. Marriage proposals do that to me."

Surrounding her as he was, he could hear her every breath, could smell her sweet, sexy scent. Felt her small tremors. Wildly protective emotions rose in him, powerful and suddenly certain. "Amber..." His arms folded around her. His mouth found its way to her ear and was heading toward her jaw when she straightened.

"I'm having enough trouble keeping my thoughts together," she said shakily, facing him, pressing her hands to her heart. "If I let you kiss me now, I don't know what will happen."

"Really?" That pleased him. "What *could* happen?"

"You know very well what."

"I want to hear you say it."

She rolled her eyes. "You know all you have to do is look at me and my thoughts scatter. I certainly can't concentrate when you put your mouth on me. I can hardly breathe."

His smile spread a bit. "Maybe you concentrate too much."

"Yes, well, it's a bad habit of mine."

"Are you ever going to answer the question?"

She drew a deep breath. "I know it's rude, but I need some air."

"You need to think."

"Yes."

Well-versed in this particular play, he followed her out, but she was stopped by Nancy at the front desk and handed a stack of messages that made her sigh.

Dax watched while she flipped through them with quick impatience. And saw her, really saw her—the weary eyes, the slight bruises beneath them, the tension in her body.

She was truly exhausted.

Nancy added a pile of files that needed immediate attention. On top of that, she placed a virtual mountain of correspondence, all of which required review and a signature.

It had to be at least a week's worth of work.

Amber took everything stoically, she even managed a smile for her employee, but Dax saw right through her.

"Put it in your office and let's go," he said quietly.

Nancy held up a finger before Amber could move. "The Garrisons. They want to see that property again."

"Terrific," Amber muttered.

"Today."

"They've seen it five times this week."

"I know. But they want to see it again and they want to see it with you."

Amber drew in a slow, purposeful breath, and Dax wondered how it was that only *he* saw her growing exhaustion. He knew how hard she worked, knew how much time Taylor demanded, and added it all up.

It equaled a breakdown for Amber.

"Call them then," she said wearily. "Tell them I'll pick them up at—"

"Tell them they can see the damn property by themselves," Dax interjected. He took the stack of work from Amber's arms. "You've done enough today. You're taking off."

Both Amber and Nancy stared at him.

"Ms. Riggs is leaving for the day," he announced for anyone listening. "She won't be back until morning."

"I will most definitely be back today," Amber said, her eyes on Dax. "I just need some air."

"You're going to get your air." Dax smiled his most charming smile. "But you won't be back today." Taking her hand in a grip of steel, he tugged her from the office.

"Dax...would you stop!" Her heels clicked noisily as she raced along beside him. "I have important business to attend to."

"You most certainly do," he assured her, ruthlessly tugging her along. "We were in the middle of something."

"I know, but I can't just leave, not now—"

"Your air," he reminded her. "You needed to get out so fast you couldn't answer my question. Remember?"

Her lips tightened, but she remained silent until they exited the building.

It was a glorious Southern California day. The sky was a deep, brilliant blue and scattered across it were little puffs of white clouds.

A picture-perfect scene.

Now if only the woman next to him could slow down enough to enjoy it.

Instead, she spun on her heels away from him and started walking.

Dax spared a moment to admire her stride. "I'm coming with you," he called.

"Like I could stop you."

He moved to keep up with her. She was pale, but never faltered. The slight wind tossed her hair, played with the hem of her skirt. Dax avoided thinking by concentrating on traffic. He avoided touching Amber by keeping his hands in his pockets.

Three blocks later, they came to a park. All green and woodsy, it had a series of trails and welcoming benches. A perfect place to ask a woman—for the third time—to marry him.

A perfect place for his future to be decided.

They were hidden from the street by trees. The sounds of birds singing drowned out any traffic they might have heard. They were alone, isolated, surrounded by beauty.

"Well," he said after a moment.

"Well."

They stared at each other stupidly, and Dax wondered if she could possibly be as attracted, as confused, as totally, irreversibly in love as he was.

Then he saw the unmistakable signs—red-rimmed eyes and damp lashes.

Dammit.

"I've thought about...you know," she said, her voice a bit ragged.

"You mean about spending the rest of your life with me?" he asked gently. "Is that why you're crying?"

She looked away. "It's been hard being a single parent. No family support, few friends. Both are my fault, but it's fact." Then she turned back to him. "Having you in my life, taking responsibility for helping with Taylor, it's been a real gift."

"But?"

"But I can't accept your offer. It's generous, kind and almost overwhelmingly irresistible, but as I told you before, I can't do it."

"Mind if I ask why?"

"It's obvious neither of us were meant for marriage."

"I don't believe that," he said softly. "And I don't believe *you* believe it. Don't chicken out here, Amber. Don't hide, not from me. Tell me the truth. I deserve that much."

"You know the truth. I'm not marriage material, and you...you like women too much to give it all up just because we have a baby."

"First of all, I stopped looking at other women the moment you came into my life."

"Which time?"

"Both," he told her grimly.

"I understand getting married is a logical solution to the unexpected unit we've become." She hugged herself. "We have a baby. We both love her with all our hearts. We're willing to share her, but the truth is, neither of us really want to be separated from her. Getting married would solve that."

"Yes," he agreed, sliding closer. "It would also solve another, deeper problem."

"Which is?"

"I want you."

"You—" She closed her eyes. "You just had me recently. A few times as a matter of fact."

The memory, as well as her tone, made him smile. "I want more than sex," he clarified. Because the admission was a new one for him, and scary, his humor vanished. "I've never said this before about anyone else, but sex with you isn't enough. I want to spend nights together. I want to *be* together. I know we started out in a whirlwind, that we've done everything backward, but let's fix it."

"Marriage won't do that, Dax."

"Why are you so resistant?"

"Because...because, dammit, it's not enough for me!" She blushed and closed her eyes. "I'm sorry. I know this sounds stupid, but to me a marriage should be about...about love. I've never thought of myself in those terms, but deep in my heart, if I'm going to do it, that's what I want."

"Love."

"That's right."

"Well that's convenient, since I happen to be madly in love with you."

"What?" She flew to her feet and stared at him as if she'd just discovered he was an alien. "What did you just say?"

He stood, too, and when she would have turned

away, he took her shoulders in his hands. She trembled. That made two of them. "I think you heard me just fine."

"I've...I've never heard those words before." Her voice was a mere whisper. She licked her lips. "I'd like to hear them again."

His heart threatened to burst out of his chest. "I love you."

"You can't."

"Why not? You're perfectly lovable."

Her mouth was open, her eyes wild. Her hand went to her chest. "Oh God. Now I can't breathe."

"Good. Neither can I." He resisted the urge to laugh because he wasn't kidding. He really couldn't breathe. "I've never said those words to a woman before, Amber."

They stared at each other.

"You're mistaken," she decided tremulously. "You have to be."

"No."

"You have no idea. I don't let people in, I'm not—"

"*Amber.*" It was so easy, so right to touch her, he thought, as his thumb gently stroked her jaw. His fingers slipped into her hair. "I've loved you from that very first day."

"But I don't know how to love you back."

"You could practice."

Moisture gathered in her beautiful eyes and she shook her head back and forth.

"Practice with me, Amber," he whispered, his heart raw.

Her eyes were huge. "I'm not ready. I need time."

"How much?"

"I don't know!"

Because she was still shaking, he gathered her stiff body close. "I'm sorry," she whispered against his chest, but her hands snaked around his neck and for a moment, she clung.

He stroked her back and tamped down any regrets. "Don't worry. It so happens, time is in plentiful supply."

And strange as it seemed, given she'd turned him down yet again, Dax felt an inkling of hope for their future.

12

THAT NIGHT, Dax lay in his bed staring at the ceiling wondering how long it would take for sleep to claim him when the phone rang.

Given how his heart picked up speed, he knew who it would be. "Hello?"

"Did you mean it?"

Amber. Unsure and unhappy. "I meant every one of those three little words," he assured her grimly.

"Another promise?"

"Another promise."

There was a long silence, and he knew she was very busy thinking.

"Have I broken one to you yet, Amber?"

"No," she said slowly, but she sounded slightly reassured. "I have to go."

His heart twisted, a feeling he was beginning to associate with her. "Good night, Amber," he whispered.

DAX FOUND Amber at what he now knew to be her favorite lunch spot. He grinned at her bowl of strawberry yogurt. "Are you going to let me watch you eat that?"

She stopped licking her spoon and eyed him over the bowl with an interesting mix of pleasure and wariness. The wariness he expected because it had been four days since he'd sought her out.

The pleasure was a nice surprise.

"No," she finally said.

Ignoring that, because whether she wanted to admit it or not, she was crazy about him, he swiveled a chair around and straddled it. Leaning forward, he took in her cool, sedate, navy blue suit. "I don't suppose I can convince you to spill again so that you could lose the uptight clothes."

Surprising him, she laughed. "Actually, I thought of you this morning when I put this on."

"Yeah?" For some reason, that gave him ridiculous pleasure. So did the thought of her standing, fresh out of a shower, naked, thinking of him.

Her voice was low. "I thought of it as my armor."

"Against?"

She played with the yogurt now. "Sometimes you give me a certain look and it makes me feel...funny."

He gave her one of those looks now and the air sizzled between them.

"That's the one," she said a bit shakily, pointing at him with her spoon. "That's it right there."

"Do you feel funny now?"

"A little, yeah."

"Me, too." He heard the rough arousal in his voice and couldn't stop himself. "And it has nothing to do with the clothes you wear." He leaned close. "You could put on real armor and it wouldn't matter one damn bit."

Her eyes closed briefly, and he knew he didn't mistake that quick flash of helpless desire on her face before she carefully masked it and rose. "I have work."

He touched her arm, stilled her. "You can believe in me, Amber. Believe in yourself enough to see it."

"I'm trying, Dax. Whatever you think of me, I want you to know that."

He rose, too, and skimmed his fingers over her cheek. "I know you've had no one to trust with yourself before, but I promise you, I'm different."

And then, because they were in the crowded café, and because neither of them were quite steady, he stepped back. "Think about it."

AMBER WANTED to do nothing but think about it. As she entered her office, her mind whirled. She moved toward her desk and the mountain of work waiting for her.

Halfway there, the earth rumbled beneath her feet. For a second she allowed herself to believe it was her overly active imagination.

It wasn't. The earthquake was short and quick, and absolutely terrifying.

There had been many this year, and she remembered each and every one of them because they'd brought on a heart-stopping panic she couldn't control.

A normal reaction for someone who'd been through what she had, she assured herself, gripping her desk, prepared to dive under it if necessary.

"It's okay," she said out loud as she waited, tense and frozen. "Just an aftershock." She knew they could occur for years after a main quake. The knowledge didn't help. Many people in the area had been terrorized by the aftershocks, not just her. It was normal.

Normal.

She told herself all of this, repeatedly, but she still forgot to breathe and her chest hurt. Her vision spotted.

And though it was over long before she even fully registered it, she remained there, rigid, heart drumming, palms damp, shaking like a leaf.

The door to her office opened and shut, and suddenly Dax was standing there, saying her name in that deep, wonderful voice.

"I came the second I felt it," he said. "I was still on the street. I thought— I didn't know how you would feel— Dammit, I hate those things!" he exclaimed, taking her arms in his strong, reassuring hands. "Are you all right?"

"Certainly." But she clung to his big, welcoming body. Just for a moment, she told herself. She'd allow herself to lean on him for just a moment. "I'm fine."

"Don't." With a gentleness that was so tender, so sweet it hurt, he curled a strand of her hair behind her ear. "Don't fake being strong for me."

"It was just an aftershock. Hardly even big enough to register on the scale."

"It registered on my scale," came his gruff reply, and for the first time she heard his breathlessness, felt the quiver in his own muscles, and realized he felt the fear, too.

She gave herself permission to hold him for another moment.

"It's okay," he whispered, gathering her tighter, absorbing her weight with ease. "We're okay."

"Taylor," she said, lifting her head. Urgency overcame her. "I want to call—"

"We will. Soon as I can remember my mother's phone number. We'll go get her together, okay? Amber, just hold onto me for a second."

We'll go get her.

We'll.

Together.

For some reason, the words softened her as nothing else could have and she let out a lungful of air, burying her face in the wonderful spot of his neck that seemed meant for her. "Don't be afraid," she told him. "I have a big, tough desk. It'll hold."

He laughed, as she had meant for him to, and somehow that softened her even more so that her arms wrapped even tighter around him.

"We're both shaking like leaves," he muttered, sinking with her to the floor. "I really hate earthquakes."

"Just for the record here," she wondered. "Who's comforting who?"

"I'm not sure, just don't let go."

She didn't. They sat huddled on the floor in each other's arms like two little children. Her legs were entwined with his, her skirt high on her thighs. His hands were on her back, slowly running up and down in a reassuring gesture that hadn't been anything but sincerely comforting, until his hands slipped beneath her jacket to the silk of her blouse.

The embrace shifted, became charged with erotic awareness, and Amber lifted her head to stare at him, into his warm eyes, then at his mouth, the one she suddenly wanted on hers. The shattering, shocking truth was, she wanted that more than she wanted her own next breath.

Dax groaned and closed his eyes. "Don't look at me like that, it's dangerous to my health."

For the life of her, she couldn't remember why she'd wanted to hold him at arm's length, couldn't remember why she was trying so hard to resist this magnetic pull she felt whenever she was with him.

Hell, she was starting to have that pull even when she *wasn't* with him.

Her arms were already around his neck, it took little movement to have her fingers fisted in his hair so that she could tug him closer, then closer still so that their mouths were a fraction of an inch apart.

"Amber." The sound of her name on his lips, spoken in that husky voice, made her heart tip on its side.

She closed the distance between them, let her eyes drift closed. Her lips parted and she felt his warm breath mingle with hers.

Her office door opened.

"Oh, excuse me," came Nancy's shocked voice.

Professionalism kept her from gawking, though Amber was certain she wanted to. After all, how often did she see her boss sprawled on the floor in a man's arms?

"I'm sorry," Nancy murmured.

Amber groaned when the door shut. She pushed away from Dax.

He let out a frustrated sigh. "I'm betting from the look on your face that what just happened is worse than the aftershock."

"I've worked hard to make sure everyone here respects me and the work I do. And in a matter of seconds, I've just ruined that image."

"Well that's pure bull."

Amber stared at him. "That's easy for you to say. You're a man, working in a man's world. You're not judged by your appearance, or who you sleep with."

"Neither are you."

"It's different here. It's highly competitive. One nasty rumor and I could be ruined."

"I see. And being caught in my arms equals a nasty rumor. Flattering."

She winced at his unusually chilly voice. "I didn't mean to insult you."

"That's the hard part, because I know it."

THAT NIGHT when Dax brought Taylor home to Amber, he made no attempt to draw her into conversation. He didn't even come in, but stood at the doorway, silently and solemnly holding Taylor close for a long moment. Arms tight around the chubby little baby, he closed his eyes and hugged her tight.

Then he lifted her high, smiled at her squeal of delight and kissed her goodbye. "I love you, baby," he whispered, and his smile was a heart-wrenching mixture of sweetness and sorrow.

All that emotion both shocked and humbled Amber to her toes. "Do you want to come in?"

He shook his head, and as if to prove his point, remained on the step as she took the diaper bag from him. He was careful not to touch her. Though she had no right to feel that way, it hurt.

She knew he was going to work. She'd seen the news. There was a fire raging in a downtown apartment building. It was filled with hundreds of trapped, terrified people, and though he rarely fought the actual fires these days, he would be on the scene. His job required it.

But she knew his distant attitude had nothing to do with that fire and everything to do with her. "Be careful tonight."

"Always." With one last, loving touch to Taylor's chubby cheek, he turned away.

"Dax."

Slowly he turned, but she didn't know what to say, how to reach him. How to make him understand.

How could she, when she didn't understand herself? "Nothing," she whispered, and then he was gone.

AMBER DID her best to keep her mind occupied for the rest of the long evening. She bathed Taylor, then read her stories, even though the baby was far more interested in chewing on the pages than listening to the words.

She even tried to do some of her own work. Nothing satisfied her and her mind drifted.

To Dax.

Desperate to distract herself, she flipped on the television, then stood riveted in horror. The downtown fire was live on all the local channels.

The flames weren't contained. Even worse, there were still people trapped on the higher levels. The city had put out the desperate call for help to neighboring counties, and though that help was on the way, for many it would be too late.

She knew Dax would never stand on the sidelines. He'd be there, in the thick of that heat, fighting for those people's lives.

Glued to the screen, she lost track of time, chewing

on her nails as she hadn't done since she was a child. When the roof of the building collapsed, she leaped to her feet, then kneeled before the television, her heart in her throat.

Three firefighters were reported missing.

She waited and waited, but they didn't give any more information, not the identities of the men or their conditions, not even after the fire was contained and then, eventually, extinguished.

No longer able to stand the not knowing, Amber turned to the phone, just as it rang.

"Honey, it's Emily McCall."

"Oh, thank goodness. Do you think you could watch Taylor for me? I have to go down."

"Oh, Amber, listen—"

"I have to go, I have to know—"

"I know, I know. But he's okay. He's not hurt. That's why I'm calling."

The relief was so overwhelming, Amber couldn't breathe. "You're sure?"

"Thomas drove down there when this mess first started, he just called me."

Dax was okay.

Amber's limbs started to shake in reaction and she collapsed onto the couch.

Emily's voice was thick with tears. "I worry about him so much. I can hear in your voice you worried, too."

"Yes. He— We— I..." She blew out a breath and tried again. "It was awful, the not knowing. I tried to imagine... Taylor needs him."

"Of course she does. What about her mother?"

"I need him, too," she said, meaning every word. "So much."

"He's my life," Emily said simply. "And so is your daughter. I'm so thankful we're all together."

The guilt that stabbed at Amber wasn't new. She felt as though she had stolen Taylor's first three months from Dax and his family and now, only a few short weeks later, couldn't imagine how she had done it.

Or why.

Her reasons for wanting to be alone hadn't made sense for hours now.

"Why don't you bring me that sweet little baby?" Emily suggested. "Then you can decide what to do."

"About what?"

Emily's voice was hushed, as if she kept a huge secret. "Well, I shouldn't say anything." This spoken in the hopeful tone of someone who wanted to be pressed.

"Please."

"Well, you know I pride myself on letting my children lead their own lives. I don't mean to be nosy."

If she hadn't been in such shock, Amber might have laughed. It was common knowledge among Dax's family exactly how wonderfully, purposely nosy Emily could be.

"But as long as you're asking," she said slyly. "I was hoping maybe *you* had something to tell *me*.

That maybe you and Dax were going to...oh, I don't know. Get married?"

Oh Lord. "Mrs. McCall—"

"Oh, no, you don't," Emily interrupted with a laugh. "Let's not go backward here. You called me Emily at the party."

"Okay. Emily—"

"Or you could just go ahead and get used to calling me Mom."

Amber's emotions were in such a tailspin, she had no control left with which to handle this situation. "I'm sorry," she managed. "But as far as wedding bells, I don't have anything to tell."

"He hasn't asked you to marry him?" Emily's disappointment sang through the line. "That boy! I taught him better than that—"

"No, no, it's not..." How to explain that *she* had screwed everything up? That there was every chance Dax no longer wanted her? "It's not his fault."

"You don't want him?"

"This is very complicated. I can't seem to think straight."

"Of course you can't! Where's my head, pressing you to talk to me before you're ready. Maybe you haven't even decided if you like me—"

Now Amber did laugh. Emily McCall could wear down a saint. "I like you, very much," she assured the older woman. "It's just that—"

"That you don't think of me as your family yet." Emily sniffed, clearly insulted. "I understand."

"You know that's not true."

"No, it's okay, you don't owe me anything."

"Emily, please. I think you're an amazing woman."

"You do?" Pleasure quickly replaced hurt. "Really?"

"Yes." It had never been easy for Amber to share herself, but for some reason, the words came now. "I think the way you love your family is beautiful."

"It's no more than any mother would do."

Maybe it was the late hour or the emotions of the day, but suddenly it was easy for Amber to admit the truth. "Not any mother."

"Not yours?"

Emily's sympathy and pity didn't frighten her as she thought it would. "Definitely not mine. But I used to dream about it, and if I could have drawn my mother the way I wanted her to be, she would have been just like you."

"Oh darling, now you're really going to make me cry."

"Don't you dare." Amber laughed through her own impending tears. "You'll get *me* started. And after what we've been through this evening, I may never stop."

"Dax is careful, you know. He's the best at what he does."

He was the best at everything he set his mind to. His work. Fatherhood. She could only imagine what a husband he'd make. The warm glow that came from that thought no longer surprised her.

"I imagine you have a lot on your mind," Emily said. "Especially with the thought of babies and marriage and all the like."

"I thought you didn't want to be nosy."

"Oh, you." But Emily had the good grace to laugh at herself. "You already have my number. Just like all my children." Her voice went stern and demanding. "Now bring me Taylor. You go to my boy."

IN THE END, Amber didn't drop off Taylor, figuring Dax would want to see her. He seemed to thrive on any opportunity to do so.

Plus she needed Taylor to hold, needed to feel that small, warm bundle of life against her, reminding her that no matter what happened with Dax, she mattered to someone.

Dax had given her a key to his house, insisting he didn't want her waiting for him outside if he was ever late when they were supposed to meet. Amber had felt uncomfortable with that, had assumed she would never use it, but it came in handy now.

Less than one minute after she arrived, Dax pulled into the driveway, setting her nerves to leaping. Head down, shoulders tense, he opened the front door and stepped inside. As if he sensed her, he stilled and slowly raised his head to reveal a weary, hollow face.

When he saw her his eyes warmed. So did Amber's heart.

13

"HEY." DAX acknowledged her, but he didn't move into the room.

Amber's nervousness tripled. Was he bothered by the fact that she'd let herself in? Was he sorry he'd given her his key?

Why didn't he say something, *anything*? "I hope you don't mind," she found herself saying awkwardly.

With an audible sigh, he kicked off his shoes.

"I...used the key you gave me."

He dropped his jacket where he stood and the leather hit the floor with a thud.

"Taylor's here, too." She felt stupid and intrusive, but a search of his expression told her nothing. A first. "Your mom offered to baby-sit, but I thought you'd want to see her."

He rolled his head on his neck, winced and then sighed again.

"If you're too tired, I'll just..."

He spoke then, though the words were muffled by the sweatshirt he was pulling off over his head. "I'm never too tired for Taylor." He tossed the sweatshirt aside, his words in direct opposition to the exhaustion on his face. "Or you, for that matter."

"Because I could just scoop her up and leave...."

He leaned back against the wall, arms crossed. "Didn't you just get here?"

"Yes."

His face was bleak, his eyes red-rimmed, and his big, tough body so weary she imagined he was standing on his feet by sheer force of will. "I saw everything on the news," she said. She watched as he dumped out the contents of his pockets into a small bowl on the low table in the entry.

His silence was killing her.

"I couldn't tear myself away from the television," she added.

He nodded and rubbed his eyes, but still didn't speak. Her heart was racing so fast she didn't know what to do.

"When the roof collapsed—" she drew a shaky breath "—and those firefighters fell through the gaping hole..."

He flinched and her heart ached at the stark pain she saw so clearly in his eyes. "Oh, Dax."

He hadn't stepped toward her, hadn't really looked at her, not once. He hadn't made one move that told her how he felt about her being there. "Would you rather I go?"

"Actually, I'm hoping you're going to tell me the real reason you're here."

"I...I thought...I just wanted to be."

He came toward her, his face still bleak and grim, but now there was something new in his gaze. He stopped a mere foot away from her. "I've never known you to stutter."

"I don't. N-n-not—" Ruthlessly she bit her tongue. "Not usually anyway." Frustrated, she reached up to shove back a loose strand of hair at the exact same moment his fingers came up to tuck it behind her ear. His hand slid over hers and he brought those joined hands to his chest. "You've been biting your nails. A new habit?"

"Another one that I've not had for years."

"What's the matter? I've never seen you so unsettled."

"Unsettled. I guess that's what you'd call worrying myself sick." All her pent-up fear spewed out. "I went through hell tonight, watching the news."

"It's my job."

"I know. *I know!* That's not what I'm saying."

"What *are* you saying?"

"That I worry, okay? I don't want to, but I do."

He let out a long breath and all the tension suddenly draining out of him, immediately replaced by a new, different sort of tension. *"Yes,"* he whispered, his eyes glittering with emotion. "Yes, *that's* what I wanted to hear."

"I suppose then, that you'd love to know I couldn't even breathe, thinking that you'd be hurt. Or worse!"

His other hand slid up her spine, around to cup

her face. His thumb brushed over her lower lip before his fingers sank into her hair, holding her head still. Closing that last gap between them, he nudged her up against his body. "Yeah. I would love to know that."

She flattened her hands against his chest and had to tip her head back to look into his eyes. "Is that ego talking?"

"No. It's not even remotely related to anything in my brain." He smoothed his hand over hers, holding it close to his chest. "It's right here, where pride has no place. And if you think you should be ashamed about worrying for me, think again. Not when I do nothing *but* think about you, worry about you, want you. It feels incredible to know you're capable of doing the same."

Had she been so selfish to keep that from him? "I care about you, Dax. So much it hurts."

For the first time that night, his eyes heated, his mouth softened. He closed his eyes and with an aching tenderness, rubbed his jaw to hers, drawing her so tight to him she could feel his every breath.

Then he pulled her even closer, burying his face in her neck. "We lost twenty-two people tonight. Six of them children. One was a baby girl, the same age as Taylor."

Shock reverberated through her and she hugged him as tight as she could. "I'm so sorry."

"I had to tell her mother—" He swallowed hard.

"I kept seeing Taylor, kept imagining how I'd feel if I had to face you, tell you that— *God*."

Envisioning the scene, Amber felt his anguish as her own. "You did everything you could, all of you did everything you could to save them."

He made a wordless sound of grief that tore at her. In her arms was the strongest, toughest, most heroic man she'd ever met, and she didn't know what to do for him. She wanted to take his pain away, wanted to hold him close so that nothing could hurt him ever again. She had no idea how long they stood there, rocking slowly, absorbing each other's heat and strength, when Taylor cried out.

"I'll get her," Dax said. "I...I need her."

Amber followed him to the room he'd set up for Taylor. It had been his office before, so the crib was between a leather sofa and an oak desk. Both were now covered with stuffed animals, toys and freshly laundered baby clothes. The place was a comfortable, cozy mess.

Taylor had fallen asleep again, on her tummy as usual, her padded bottom sticking up in the air, her fist in her mouth.

Dax stood by the crib, his hand on Taylor's back, a look of combined sorrow and joy on his face, so poignant it hurt to look at him. But that wasn't a good enough reason to turn away.

For the first time in her life, Amber reached out and made the first move. It was difficult, but only until she touched him. At the contact with his warm, hard body it was the most natural thing in the world to slip her hands around his waist and hug him from behind. "She's okay, Dax."

He nodded and turned, gathering her close. The exhaustion was still there in his expression, but some of the bleak despair seemed to have lifted. That it was herself and Taylor doing that for him gave her a warm burst of something so thrilling, so breathtaking, so wild and fierce, it terrified her.

It was *hope.*

Was it real? Could it last?

Dax leaned past her, stroked a gentle hand down Taylor's back and with an achingly tender expression, bent and kissed his baby, murmuring something Amber couldn't hear.

Straightening, he looked deep into Amber's eyes as a slow, unbearably sad smile crossed his mouth.

Then he left the room.

Confused, she followed him as he padded down the hallway to his own bedroom.

He didn't turn on the light, but she made out his silhouette as he tugged off his shirt and let it fall. His shoulders slumped as he stood there in the middle of the room, still and silent.

"Dax?"

"I'm fine," he said, emotionlessly. "You don't have to stay."

The only light in the room came from the pale moon shining through the window, so she couldn't see his expression. She didn't have to in order to know he felt empty to the core. "You want me to go?"

A harsh laugh escaped him. "No. But I know you're still afraid of all this, and I'm just vulnerable enough tonight to beg."

"I can't help the fear, Dax," she said carefully. "It's all a part of it for me. But I can tell you what I feel for you is different than anything I've ever felt before."

She felt his surprise.

She closed her eyes for a moment and pressed her fingertips to them while she drew in a deep breath. "I won't deny what's between us, but I feel like I'm on an emotional roller coaster."

"I understand that you like to keep your emotions in check. Hell, you've had to in order to survive, but Amber..." He lifted his broad shoulders helplessly. "I can't do the same."

In the dark his silhouette seemed larger than life, more vital, more full of passion and hope than she could ever be, and never had she felt the lack in herself so much as she did in that moment. "I know," she whispered.

"I won't ever hurt you," he said quietly. "I've told you that. But I can't temper myself, hide my emotions. No matter how much I want you, I can't change. Not even for you."

He was close enough now that she could see him more clearly. The contours of his bare chest were delineated by the faint moon's glow. He was powerful, and he was beautiful.

And he could be hers.

All she had to do was believe it.

He turned away and sank down onto his huge bed. With a little groan, he flopped on his back and covered his face with one arm.

Exhaustion had clearly claimed him.

Was it too late to tell him? Could she find both the courage and the words? "Dax?"

He let out an answering grunt, but didn't budge.

She moved close, until her knees bumped the mattress. She lifted one to the bed and bent over him, gently setting a hand on his bare chest.

At the unexpected heat of him, she nearly pulled back, but the sensation of skin to skin felt so good, she set her other hand on him as well. Then closed her eyes to savor it.

Suddenly his hands came up, tugged her down. Gasping in surprise, she fell over him.

"If you're going to lean over me, staring as I sleep," he muttered, "then at least get down here and keep me company while you're doing it."

Those were the last words he spoke. He drew her close, tucked himself around her, then immediately fell into a deep, exhausted slumber.

He was warm and safe and strong. There was no way to resist snuggling in even closer.

Then she, too, fell asleep.

SHE DREAMED they made love...she could feel him, all of him, skin to skin, burning her, healing her, making her body hum.

She dreamed of his hands skimming over her body, shedding her clothes. The picture was so vivid she could feel the calluses on his fingertips when he touched her bare flesh with such terrifying tenderness it made her weep and press closer.

She dreamed she touched him, too, and under her hands the muscles of his big, tough body quivered. In his eyes she saw need and ecstasy and anguish and oh...

This was no dream.

"You're awake." Indecision and sweet resignation swam in his eyes.

They'd already established she wasn't a morning person, nothing had changed. Then she realized it wasn't morning yet. She blinked in confusion because she was wrapped around him like a blanket.

"I woke up like this," he murmured. "We must have gravitated toward each other in our dreams."

He expected her to walk away. She could hear it in his voice. He thought she'd made a decision about him, about her life, and that decision didn't involve him.

He thought wrong.

"Touch me, Dax."

The strain on his face nearly broke her heart. "I am."

"More."

"It won't change anything," he said tightly. "We'll

Jill Shalvis 195

still be fundamentally at odds, wanting different things, and—"

She shifted closer to that intriguing, throbbing heat pressing between her legs. "Mmm." She grabbed his hands from her hips and slid them over her body. To her waist, her ribs, her breasts.

"Amber." He groaned. "You feel incredible, but—"

"You talk too much." She kissed him softly, then not so softly, drawing him in deeper, and he let out a tortured sigh, deepening the kiss himself. As if he could read her mind, her dream, her need, he caressed her, worshipped her body and set her senses on fire.

"My clothes," she managed as his mouth dipped and nipped over her collarbone, trailing to a breast. His tongue circled her bare nipple, and she arched closer. "Where did my clothes go?" She moaned when his hot, pulsing erection nudged at her wet center. *"Where did yours go?"*

"We must have shed them in the night."

He rose above her, swirling that inventive, greedy tongue over her other breast, teasing the nipple until she nearly cried.

When she tried to lift up her legs and draw him inside her, he evaded her, slipping down her body. She felt his warm breath high on the inside of her thigh. Equal parts thrill and fear coursed through her. "Um...Dax?"

"Shh. You talk too much." His tongue swirled

over her. Then his teeth, and when he sucked her into his mouth, he made her wild, frantic. Shameless. And as the orgasm tore through her, he took her to heights she'd never even imagined.

Unbelievably, he would have rolled away then, but she managed to open her eyes and saw his vulnerability, and understood he appreciated hers.

He wouldn't take advantage of her.

She felt the resolute, unmistakable connection of their hearts and souls, and knew he never could. She reversed their positions, holding him in place as she slowly and torturously experimented on his body with her mouth.

When he tossed back his head, his face tight in a mask of agonized pleasure, she lifted her mouth off of him and licked her lips.

He moaned.

"Am I doing all right?" she whispered.

"You're doing better than all right," he managed in a strangled voice. "And if you stop now, there's every chance I'm going to die on the spot."

Empowered, she gave him a wicked grin before resuming.

In less than two minutes, she had him clawing at the sheets, shaking, begging for release. The thrill of that was such a rush she nearly came from just watching him.

"Love me," she whispered.

"I do." His eyes squeezed shut, hiding himself from her. "Amber—"

"Condom?"

She saw him hesitate, and desperate for the feel of him thick and throbbing inside her, she reared up and opened his nightstand herself.

He made a rough sound, reached past her and grabbed a foil packet. With a new boldness, she took it and attempted to put the thing on, but it wasn't nearly as easy as it seemed it should be. "It's not big enough," she said, surprised when he let out a groaning laugh.

"Amber, stop. This isn't—"

Before he could deny her, she drew his face down to hers, arching her hips as she kissed him, forcing his decision.

A low groan came from deep in his throat, and he barely managed to get the condom on before he thrust into her, hard and deep. "I'm sorry." His voice was as rough and ragged as his breathing. But he held her hips and thrust again.

She wanted to tell him not to be sorry, that this was what she wanted, but all she could do was cry out with the pleasure of him inside her. She tossed back her head and gave him everything she had, and as she did, her heart opened, rejoiced, and in return, received.

When it was over, when she lay limp and exhausted in his arms, their bodies still connected and pulsing with the passion and love they'd shared, she smiled for the first time in too long as she drifted back off into sleep.

Dax held Amber in his arms long afterward, listening to her soft, deep breathing, watching her relaxed face. Though he relished the sight of her sprawled against him, though he soaked in each and every lush curve and all the feminine roundness that so turned him on, he almost wished she'd put on some clothes, because even the feel of her creamy, soft skin against his made him want her again.

He had the feeling he would always want her.

The yearning for her spread within him and he pulled her even closer, needing to take what he could before she woke all the way up this time, and remembered she wasn't ready.

It took every bit of restraint he had to keep from kissing her awake, to keep from trying to convince her that what they shared was so incredibly right.

How could she not know?

Or maybe that was it. She *did* know, and the reality was too frightening.

Her body certainly hadn't had any such reservations. She'd given all of herself, holding nothing back. The way she'd held him, stroked him, the way she'd looked at him, had spoken clearly of her heart's desires.

His own heart raced in remembered response.

He'd never, in all his thirty-two years, been touched the way she'd touched him. She wasn't experienced, no one with that much wonder and awe in her eyes at the simplest of his kisses could be experienced, but she had a surprisingly sensuous, earthy streak and was such a quick study that he got hard just remembering.

He enjoyed everything about her; the easy intelligence in her eyes, her sweet, warm laughter, the wonderful way she mothered Taylor.

Leaving her would be the hardest thing he'd ever had to do, but there was no choice. He was in love with her. Hopelessly, irrevocably in love. It was his first time, but he knew himself, knew that he'd do everything in his power to insure this went his way. He would seduce, cajole and convince her—whatever it took—that they belonged together.

He would probably eventually succeed.

But it would be no good unless Amber decided for herself that they belonged together. No good because he'd never know if it was the path she would have chosen for herself.

In her sleep, she frowned and whimpered, and the sound went through him like a knife. "Shh," he whispered, soothing her with his hands and voice. "I've got you."

Immediately she stilled. The frown faded. So did much of her tension. Her soft, warm breath tickled the skin of his neck. Her feet were snuggled against his, soaking up their warmth and her hands rested trustingly against his chest. Even their hearts beat in unison, he could feel the rhythm echoing through him.

He missed her already, and though he needed to

get some sleep, he didn't want to close his eyes, didn't want to miss a minute of this.

God, it hurt, the letting go, but in the end, he could do little else.

AMBER AWOKE to the sound of Taylor's cooing in the next room. It was a happy sound and she smiled.

Until she realized she was in Dax's warm, welcoming bed. Alone. She stretched, looking for him, and at the sight of a note on his pillow, her heart stopped.

> Dear Amber,
>
> I had to get back to work.
>
> I'll be busy for several days, maybe more, before I can get another day off. Please, if you can, let my parents have my days with Taylor. They love her and will take care of her.
>
> You can trust them, Amber.
>
> 　　　　　　　　　　　　　　Love, Dax

You can trust them. He apparently thought she didn't know that, and had to be told.

Her own fault, she admitted, closing her eyes. She'd done a good job of letting him think that she was incapable of trust, period.

With a soft groan, she lay back and listened to Taylor's joyous babbling. It should have felt right to wake up in his bed, it *would* have felt right, if he'd been there.

She'd let him think what they shared was purely physical, let him assume the problems between them were insurmountable. She'd hurt him, and that knowledge was an anguish she'd have to face.

And somehow fix.

14

SHE WAS A COWARD. Not an easy admission, but Amber wouldn't shy away from the truth.

Somewhere along the road, she'd accepted that Dax really did love her. It was a miracle, and it still made her marvel, but she accepted it.

She also accepted that she felt the same.

But she hadn't told him, and that was inexcusable. The words had fairly screamed from her heart last night and she'd kept them to herself. Selfish and afraid, she'd held them near and dear, where they could do little good.

He deserved to know.

It wasn't exactly complimentary that it had taken her so long to really *get* it, but she could face that, too. She'd been hiding. She'd kept herself from living her life to its fullest because she was afraid.

That was going to change.

Last night had been a turning point for her, and if she was being honest, she also had to admit her transformation hadn't started last night. It had begun a year before in a dark, dirty basement where she'd faced her mortality.

She'd changed.

She'd learned love didn't have to hurt, that she could indeed trust someone other than herself. Dax needed to know that, too, and he needed to be thanked for teaching her that lesson, but before she could even begin to do that, she had to make him understand how much he meant to her.

But he wasn't home, and if he was at work, he wasn't returning her calls. It might have taken her too long, but she'd found the depth of her true feelings for him and she wouldn't give up. She could do this, she could fight for what she wanted.

And what she wanted was Dax McCall in her life, in her home, in her heart.

Forever.

SINCE DAX had made himself so thoroughly scarce and unavailable, Amber was forced to start with something else. Something she'd been wanting to do for awhile.

It required only a trip to the county recorder's office.

She gave Taylor Dax's last name.

They both deserved that, father and daughter, and she wanted Taylor to be a McCall. She thought Dax wanted that, too, and doing it felt right, very right.

There was something else she wanted to do, and while she waited to talk to Dax, she went for that as well. It was tough, and meant swallowing a lot of pride, but it was for Taylor.

Her father answered the phone in his usual gruff,

booming voice, and when he heard Amber, he became all the more gruff. "What do you want?"

As she had all of her life, Amber went on the defensive, and strove to cover that with icy coolness. "You told Dax you wanted to see your granddaughter. Was that true?"

"Yes." He cleared his throat, a sign of unease. But her father was never uneasy.

Could he be as nervous as she?

There was a time in Amber's life when she would have been agonizing over this, wishing he would show just the slightest interest, give her one little word of encouragement.

Suddenly—or maybe not so suddenly at all—it didn't matter. She ached for his presence in her life, solely for Taylor's sake now.

Yes, she still wanted a father who approved of her and what she'd done with her life. But she'd learned she was fine without that approval. Better than fine. "Have you changed your mind?"

"Actually, it was more than that."

"I don't understand," she said slowly.

His voice was harsh. Gruff as ever. Irritated. "Can't a man see his only daughter, as well?"

"Me?"

"You hard of hearing, Amber?"

There was no softening in his tough attitude. There came no words of apology or any request for forgiveness. She understood she'd never get that, but it didn't stop her sudden smile. "No, of course not."

Amazement gave way to a tentative peace. "You can see us whenever it suits you."

"Well, it suits me."

It suited her, too, and after he'd hung up, Amber reflected on her life, where it was going, and she smiled again.

DAX KNEELED in the destruction and ash of the burned-out apartment building, taking notes. His investigation was in full swing.

But he was no closer to finding the arsonist now then he had been four days ago. Swearing to himself, he stared down at his pad, but he couldn't see a single word. He'd worked himself to near exhaustion.

He'd had to.

The arsonist, whoever he was, was now wanted for more than starting the fire. He would have to be accountable for all the destruction he'd caused, and for the waste of human life.

Murder.

Finding him or her would depend on Dax and how good his investigation was. But damn, it was hard to keep his head straight when his heart hurt. He truly hadn't expected to fall in love, it just hadn't been part of his grand plan. But it was done, there was nothing he could do about it, except go on with his life.

He'd been at work so long his eyes were grainy. The fierce pounding in his head was probably due to lack of food; he couldn't remember when he'd last had a meal. But if he slowed down enough to eat, then his brain would kick in again and he'd be back to ground zero, mooning pathetically over a woman he couldn't have and missing the daughter he wanted to hug with all his heart.

Disgusted with himself, he lurched to his feet. He was doing no good here. He drove to his office, where he intended to read and reread all the reports until he could figure out what he was missing. Then he'd go to his mom's and hold his daughter for awhile.

His office looked like a disaster zone, which was defeating. The desk was piled high with files and other reports, many of which had fallen to the floor, next to a bag of diapers.

For the first time in his career, he stood at the doorway, thinking about the job he loved with all his heart and felt...overwhelmed.

And hungry, damn hungry.

It wasn't a stretch to use that hunger as an excuse to make his way to the kitchen.

There was always food in a fire station, wasn't there? It felt good to be able to count on something, he thought in a rare moment of self-pity. But while there was food in the refrigerator, none of it was prepared.

He went into the connecting room, the "great room," the men called it because of its size. There was a big screen television on its last legs, several couches—all of which had seen better days—a scarred but functional dining room set, and their pride and joy—a pool table.

"Hey!" he called out. "Who's cooking lunch?"

The two on-duty men watching soap operas didn't budge.

The two playing pool kept up their game. Through the open window he could plainly see two more men standing outside where they'd just finished washing their rigs.

No one answered, or so much as glanced his way.

Dax wasn't insulted, he knew all too well why he was being ignored. They had a tacit agreement. It wasn't necessarily a fair one, but it was simple.

He who got hungry first, cooked.

The last one to eat cleaned up.

Most people thought firefighters ate so fast because they were always trying to keep one step ahead of the fire bell. Not true.

They just didn't want to do dishes.

"So nobody's hungry," he said dryly.

Nobody moved.

Of course not. If they answered in the affirmative, then they'd have to cook. If they said no, then they couldn't eat whatever he cooked.

It was tricky, and if he'd been in a more generous mood, he'd have better appreciated the humor. But he had no humor left. "Damn," he muttered and turned back to the kitchen. The laughter that broke out behind him made him swear even more colorfully.

But he cracked the refrigerator open again. He'd lost fair and square.

A nap might have better suited him than preparing spaghetti sauce for the entire gang, but he was stubborn as well as hungry. Cranking up the radio on the counter, he chopped up a green pepper and tried to stay in the moment.

Tried to stay out of his past.

Tried to stay out of the part of his brain that hurt.

The loud, hard, pulsing rock blaring from the radio helped. So did all the food he popped into his mouth instead of into the pot.

But he kept coming back to one thing...Amber had asked him for more time, for some space. It was all she'd ever asked of him.

And he hadn't given it.

The selfishness of that, the pure greed of it, had him stopping in his tracks, a forgotten knife in one hand, a mushroom in the other.

When had he become so rigid, so unyielding?

Disgusted with himself, he chopped more vegetables with a vengeance, nearly slicing off a finger.

He *would* give her what she wanted, and while it was all fresh in his mind, he yanked the telephone off its hook and dialed her number to tell her so.

When he got her machine, he hung up, frustrated. Fine. She could have her damn time. But he wouldn't let her go. *Couldn't* let her go.

His ears played a cruel trick on him then. He

thought he could hear her voice. To block it out, he cranked up the volume on the radio.

He could still hear her.

Another vicious crank of the dial helped, barely. His ears rang. The floor vibrated with the beat. The windows rattled.

In unison, he heard the guys bellow for him to lower the volume, but he ignored them and had to smile at the irony.

He could still hear her.

One last touch to the radio and he had the volume maxed out.

Ahh, he thought...peace. *Finally.* Maybe now he could get some damn food into his gnawing gut.

Satisfied, he grabbed a tomato and froze.

She was standing there, or at least he was dreaming that she was. Rubbing his eyes ruthlessly, he blinked the gritty exhaustion away and looked again.

She was still there in the doorway of the kitchen, hands braced on the jamb on either side of her as she looked at him with an unreadable expression on her face.

His heart stopped, then kicked in again with a painfully slow thudding. The clothes she wore were unlike her, softer, more feminine, and incredibly, unwittingly sexy. He couldn't tear his gaze away. The long, flowing, flowery dress was tight in the bodice and flared gently at her hips before falling nearly to her ankles. There was a row of tiny, dainty buttons down the front, starting at the mouthwatering spot just between her full breasts.

She'd never looked so lovely.

God, he wished she was his.

15

DAX TOLD HIMSELF to cool it. She was probably here to go over something about Taylor, and he wondered how he would live through all the *time* he'd vowed to give her.

She sent him a tentative smile and raised her eyebrows at the music.

With a flick of his wrist, he turned off the radio. The silence was nearly as deafening as the music had been. "Taylor—?" he asked.

"She's fine," Amber said quickly. "She's with your mom."

He nodded, then said gruffly, "I miss her."

She clasped her hands together, but other than that, remained perfectly still. "I know. I...wanted to talk to you."

Great. How was he going to keep from grabbing her and holding on tight? He realized he still held the knife and a tomato, and he set them both down, wiping his hands on a towel because he had to keep them busy. "I'm making lunch."

A smile flickered across her firm, unpainted mouth. Had he ever seen her without lipstick? Yes, he remembered with a violent reaction in his lower body. She'd been sleeping in his bed at the time, a satisfied, cat-in-cream smile on those naked lips.

"I didn't realize you could cook," she said. "Or that you'd..." She trailed off, her voice steady enough, but he could see the telltale sign of a blush creeping up her cheeks.

Interesting. She didn't seem so in control now. "Or that I'd what?"

She lifted a shoulder. "Look so good doing it."

Unfortunately, sweet as that admission was, it only made his ache more pronounced.

The awkward silence settled again and Amber took a step toward him. "I'm sorry to intrude, but I haven't been able to reach you."

"Yeah. About that..."

"Don't be sorry," she said quickly. "I know you've been busy."

Which wasn't exactly the reason he hadn't called or gone by to see her. "Yes, I've been busy," he said carefully, stepping around the counter to face her. "But I've also been a jerk. I should have gotten back to you, but frankly, I was too busy being selfish."

"Selfish?" She laughed at that. "You? I doubt that, Dax."

"I promised not to push, I promised to be patient, and I couldn't do either. I can do better. I can give you your time and space."

"Dax—"

"But I can't let you go. You should know that up front."

"It's okay—"

"No, dammit, it's not."

"Dax—"

"Let me finish. For the first time in my life I broke a promise and I'm sorry for that, so sorry."

"Oh, Dax." Misery crossed her face. "Don't apologize, that's not what I came here for. I wanted to tell you..." She looked at her feet for a long moment before lifting her head again. "I have come to a conclusion," she said in a businesslike tone.

He swallowed. "That sounds bad."

"No." The sophistication fled. "It's just so much harder to tell you than I imagined, and truthfully, I imagined it being pretty tough."

His heart sank. "You can tell me anything, Amber. You know that."

Clearly filled with pent-up energy, she slowly walked the room. "You've been in my head a long time now, Dax."

"Uh...okay." *That was good, right?*

Her back to him, she studied the wall, which was covered in pictures. The guys had been pinning up photos ever since the station first opened ten years before. There were families, girlfriends, boyfriends, kids...an entire ten years worth of living.

What did she see? he wondered. *What did she feel?* He wished he knew.

"I know it seems silly," she said to the wall. "To tell you that I can't stop thinking of you."

"I understand perfectly."

She turned to him then. "It's really quite maddening."

He nodded. Definitely maddening.

"You're different, you know. Different from anyone I've ever known."

"Is that different good, or different bad?"

She smiled a full-blown smile that took his breath. "I learned things from you. I learned I didn't have to be strong all the time, that I *could* lean on someone else once in awhile. I can be independent, Dax, and still let someone in."

"Someone?"

She laughed. *Laughed.* "You, silly. I let *you* in."

While he stood there with his mouth open, staring stupidly, she came toward him, smile still in place, her gaze tentative. "I learned to trust you. To let you trust me." Her warm, loving eyes touched him first, then her hands when she stepped close enough to set them on his chest. "And I realized something else, and this is the biggie..." Those clever hands slid up his chest and cupped his face. "I was afraid. I knew and understood that. What I didn't know, or understand, Dax, was *your* fear."

She curled her fingers in his hair, holding him when he might have stepped back and denied her. "The truth is Daxton McCall, despite your bravado and tough words, you're every bit as scared as I am."

Behind them, the swinging door to the kitchen opened as two of the firefighters stuck their heads in.

"Not that we're admitting anything," one said.

"But we're looking for food— *Oh.* Excuse me." He straightened with a new, more charming smile when he saw Amber. "I didn't realize we had company."

"*You* don't," Dax said, his eyes still on Amber. "Get out."

"But how about lunch?" asked the other one, shoving his buddy aside and sniffing theatrically. "Something smells good." He winked at Amber. "Or is that you?"

Dax growled at them, and they both quickly backed out.

Amber looked appalled. "Dax! That's no way to treat—"

"Say it again," he demanded, reaching for her, giving her a little shake. He didn't know whether to allow this glimmer of hope within him, and the not knowing was killing him. "Say it!"

"That you obviously need some etiquette classes, or that you're a chicken?"

He grated his teeth. "The chicken part."

"Oh, I think you heard me." Dropping her hands from him, she sashayed away to the counter, and picked up his knife. She hacked at a tomato. "You really changed things for me." Her words were a tad uneven, but her hands were a blur as she demolished the tomato. "You taught me so much about how I could feel for people, about how people could feel for me..."

He came around behind her, sliding his hands along her expressive arms to hold them still. In the interest of both their fingers, he gently set down the knife. "I can't dispute the chicken part," he admitted. Wrapping his arms around her, he held her tight, buried his face in her neck. God, he loved her so much. He turned her to face him. "It's true, I used your resistance to reinforce my own. I don't know what I expected would happen between us, but it certainly wasn't for me to fall so deep."

Her eyes filled and she opened her mouth, but he softly set a finger to her lips. "Yes, the thought of a future with just one woman terrified me more than anything I'd ever faced, but I knew there was no other woman for me, *anywhere*, and there never would be again."

"Oh, Dax." A tear spilled over and he gently swiped it off with his thumb.

"I fell in love with you, Amber," he said huskily. "And I fell good and hard. That was the easy part. The hard part came later, when I realized you didn't feel the same way, and that you might never feel the same. I'm sorry I hurt you, I never meant to."

"I know."

Because he could, he pulled her close and wondered what was going to happen.

"I called my father," she said. "I'm going to see him. For Taylor." She lifted her head from his chest and stroked his jaw as she looked deep into his eyes. "I also changed Taylor's last name, officially, to McCall. I thought that was important."

His heart swelled, but before he could even attempt to tell her how much it meant to him, she dropped her hands from him. "That's part of why I came here today. I wanted you to know what I had done."

That was it? Hello. Let me drive you crazy. See ya?

Her smile wobbled and she carefully stepped back from him. "Well..." She whirled and walked quickly to the door while his heart died a thousand deaths.

Then, before she turned the handle, she hesitated. Killing him.

"Aren't you even going to try and stop me?" She whirled around to look at him. "You realize I have no idea what I'm doing! I could really use some help here."

His heart leaped into his throat, but before he could say a word, she lifted a hand. "No, wait. Don't help me. That's not right. I'm the one who has to do this, not you."

"Amber..." Had he missed something? "Honey, are you making any sense?"

She drew a deep breath. "Dammit, Dax, I love you, too." Her smile shook badly. "How's that for sense?"

Stunned, all he could do was nod. "It's good."

"I guess I'll have to prove it to you." She swung open the double doors of the kitchen and cleared her throat.

Six curious men turned their heads.

"Listen up everyone..." She looked at Dax over her shoulder. "I love Dax McCall."

Wild cheers, lewd whistles and a chorus of catcalls greeted this announcement. Amber grinned. "Did everyone get that?"

More cheers.

She slammed the doors on them and turned back to Dax, who was still standing there, mouth open, heart pounding, love and shock singing through his veins.

"I meant it," she said quietly, once again clasping her hands together. Her smile was still very shaky and her eyes suspiciously wet. "I really meant it. Now I dare you to be more trusting, to lay more on the line than that!"

Oh, he was up for the challenge, yes he was. With his own shaky smile, he stalked past her and yanked open the kitchen doors. "Okay another announcement...I'm forsaking bachelorhood—"

Loud groans greeted that announcement, which made him laugh. "I'm getting something better, trust me."

Someone called out something about getting lucky every single night with the same woman and Dax grinned. "That, too, but more importantly, I'm going to marry Amber, and spend every single day of the rest of my life a very happy man."

Next to him, Amber gasped. "*Marry?*"

He hauled her close. "Love conquers all, we know that. We belong together. Say you'll marry me, Amber. Say you'll give me forever."

In tune to the renewed catcalls, laughter and cheers of congratulations, Amber laughed and went up on tiptoe to kiss him. In soft agreement, she said, "Yes, I'll give you forever."

COMING SOON...

AN EXCITING
OPPORTUNITY TO SAVE
ON THE PURCHASE OF
HARLEQUIN AND
SILHOUETTE BOOKS!

*DETAILS TO FOLLOW
IN OCTOBER 2001!*

YOU WON'T WANT TO MISS IT!

PHQ401

Harlequin truly does
make any time special. ...
This year we are celebrating
weddings in style!

To help us celebrate, we want you to tell us how wearing the Harlequin wedding gown will make your wedding day special. As the grand prize, Harlequin will offer one lucky bride the chance to **"Walk Down the Aisle"** in the Harlequin wedding gown!

There's more...

For her honeymoon, she and her groom will spend five nights at the **Hyatt Regency Maui.** As part of this five-night honeymoon at the hotel renowned for its romantic attractions, the couple will enjoy a candlelit dinner for two in Swan Court, a sunset sail on the hotel's catamaran, and duet spa treatments.

To enter, please write, in, 250 words or less, how wearing the Harlequin wedding gown will make your wedding day special. The entry will be judged based on its emotionally compelling nature, its originality and creativity, and its sincerity. This contest is open to Canadian and U.S. residents only and to those who are 18 years of age and older. There is no purchase necessary to enter. Void where prohibited. See further contest rules attached. Please send your entry to:

Walk Down the Aisle Contest

In Canada
P.O. Box 637
Fort Erie, Ontario
L2A 5X3

In U.S.A.
P.O. Box 9076
3010 Walden Ave.
Buffalo, NY 14269-9076

You can also enter by visiting www.eHarlequin.com
Win the Harlequin wedding gown and the vacation of a lifetime!
The deadline for entries is October 1, 2001.

HARLEQUIN®
Makes any time special ®

PHWDACONT1